He grinned at her.

Her heart seemed to skip a beat at the warmth of his smile. Her reaction was wholly inappropriate for the situation and she had to ignore how attractive the man was. He was her client. Not to mention a prince.

"I felt the same way when I first saw the caves. Come around here, please," he said, indicating his side of the table where schematics were laid out in front of him. "This shows where the caves are on Adysarina island. My favorite sculpture is in this cave." He indicated with his finger. "Cave six. It's a little bit off the beaten path, so if we did open it to the public, we would have to create a new roadway. I think it will be worth it. We could start with it, but I think I'll build up your anticipation before I take you there."

"Oh, will you be coming with me?"

Her heart started to race again at the thought of getting to talk with him, hear his ideas and stories about the island, laugh with him, be close to him.

Dear Reader,

One of my favorite parts of being an author is all the research I get to do. I loved exploring Priya's passion for her work as a conservator. I only wish some of the caves and murals I describe in *Cinderella's Forbidden Prince* existed. But the Ajanta and Ellora Caves are fortunately real. I was a teenager when I saw the awe-inspiring paintings and rock-cut sculptures. They really are incredible. A return visit is definitely on my travel list.

I've always wanted to write about royalty, so I was really excited to have the chance to write a Cinderella story set on a fictional island kingdom.

With Priya and Rohan's story, I wanted to fully embrace the fairy tale. Priya has grown up believing she isn't worthy of being loved. She needs someone open with his feelings to show her that isn't true. Rohan is the strong, honorable prince ready to do his duty for the improvement of his country. Their connection is instantaneous, but at times it seems as though they aren't ultimately destined to be together. It takes a strong couple like Priya and Rohan to fight together for the future they deserve.

I hope you enjoy my modern fairy tale.

Love,

Ruby

Cinderella's Forbidden Prince

Ruby Basu

Recycling programs
for this product may
not exist in your area.

ISBN-13: 978-1-335-73699-4

Cinderella's Forbidden Prince

Copyright © 2023 by Ruby Basu

Harlequin Enterprises ULC
22 Adelaide St. West, 41st Floor
Toronto, Ontario M5H 4E3, Canada
www.Harlequin.com

Printed in U.S.A.

Ruby Basu lives in the beautiful Chilterns with her husband, two children and the cutest dog in the world. She worked for many years as a lawyer and policy lead in the civil service. As the second of four children, Ruby connected strongly with *Little Women*'s Jo March and was scribbling down stories from a young age. She loves creating new characters and worlds.

Books by Ruby Basu

Harlequin Romance

Baby Surprise for the Millionaire

Visit the Author Profile page
at Harlequin.com for more titles.

For Dev and El, who are my world

CHAPTER ONE

PRIYA SEN REVIEWED her file with the notes detailing the preservation and restoration project for the fourth time that morning. She'd already read them ten times a day since finding out, a week ago, she would be taking over the role of leader of the conservation team working on the murals in the royal palace on Adysara, a little-known island country off the coast of India.

It was safe to say she already had the information committed to memory. But one last look over wouldn't hurt.

It was barely seven o'clock, but Priya had already been up for two hours. She'd woken to the sounds of unfamiliar bird calls.

It had been late evening when she'd arrived on Adysara the previous day. She'd been exhausted after the fourteen-hour flight from England, followed by a two-hour ferry ride from India. Once she'd finally arrived at the building her co-workers were living in for the duration of the project, she barely had the energy to say hello to the others before flopping onto her bed and falling into a deep sleep.

She woke up refreshed, rejuvenated and earlier than anyone else. She'd got ready, then rushed outside to breathe the island air. She immediately felt the sense of homecoming she always experienced whenever she was in India. Technically, Adysara wasn't India and, technically, she was a foreigner, having been born and brought up in England, but something about this place claimed her. She felt like she belonged—something she'd never felt growing up.

Now, after a quick breakfast of luchi and eggs, she was desperate to get to the palace and have her first look at the murals she'd pored over in photos.

Her group's quarters were in a wooded area about a mile's walk from the palace, no doubt to make sure they were hidden from the view of the royal family. Although the team had a minivan, Priya was too excited to wait an hour until it would depart. Clutching the folder with nervous fingers, she walked towards the palace.

It was only when the path took her out of the woods she saw the palace up close and

personal for the first time. Four storeys of
carved granite with large arched windows
at every level. It was magnificent—and this
was only the side view where the staff entered. She'd seen the front in pictures with its
large central marble dome covering an indoor
courtyard. The eighteenth-century architecture in the front and rear with its archways
and turrets could rival Mysore Palace.

She held her breath as she walked through
the door, half expecting the security guards
to apprehend her immediately and remove
her from the premises.

Once inside the palace, Priya could see a
wide stone staircase on her right. She knew
this would lead up to the back of the ball-
rooms and reception areas which were usually open to the public. Her team would be
in some of those rooms since they wanted to
protect the integrity of the murals and were
working in situ.

In front of her, there was a rabbit warren of
corridors with several doors, and more corridors, leading off them. These must lead to
rooms used by the palace workers and somewhere, down one of the passageways would be
a room for preparing the chemicals her team
would be using, and there would be another

room, which would be climate-controlled, where the art restoration was being performed.

She'd done conservation projects in stately homes before but nothing as grand as this. Only in her wildest dreams would she have imagined someone like her working there.

Doubts assailed her. She had no right to be there. She was a fraud. She was only there because her colleague had to return to England for a family emergency.

'Ah, Priya. There you are.' Her boss and head conservator, Toby 'Mac' MacFarlane came up behind her. 'I knew you'd want to get here early. Are you ready?'

Priya swallowed. Was she ready? This was the biggest job her company, Courtham Conservation Services, had ever undertaken. If they completed it successfully, they would probably be able to pick and choose what they worked on in future. And where.

If she could stay as team leader or be considered as a lead on future projects around India or the rest of the world, her professional aspirations would be fulfilled.

The role she was replacing was crucial to the project's success. She may not have been the first choice for it, but she was more than qualified to take over. She knew the details of the project. She could do this.

Couldn't she?

There was no time for self-doubt to creep in. She had to prove she was capable.

Priya breathed in deeply, straightening her shoulders. 'I'm ready,' she said. 'Lead the way.'

As they walked through the rooms of the palace, Mac pointed out where other teams were working. Members of her company had been working in the palace for months already and had concentrated first on the areas and rooms that would be used extensively for events for a gala taking place in two months. Initially the whole group had worked on the art restoration to ensure the areas were completed in time. Now, although there were still some pieces to finish off, the group had been split into separate project teams and she would be leading the conservation work on the palace murals and stone carved sculptures while other teams dealt with the painting restorations.

Finally, Mac led her to the mural she would be preserving for the next few weeks.

Priya might be an expert in conservation, but the first time she saw a piece of art in person she could never view it with a technical eye. She could only stand and marvel at it.

And the wall painting in front of her, depicting a royal family picnicking in a forest watched by various animals, was more magnificent than any photo or video could do justice with its vibrant colours and detailed brushwork.

But she couldn't just stand around admiring the piece—there wasn't any time to waste if her team wanted to get this area completed before the gala.

Priya had a quick meeting with her team, making sure she knew everyone's activities for the day. She already knew the majority of her colleagues since they were employed directly by her company, but there were four people who had been seconded from different organisations to build on the interdisciplinary nature of the job.

Her predecessor had taken an approach which divided the mural into sections at various stages of preservation. Priya decided to float between the sections during the day so she could observe the flow of work generally, but she could move easily if one section needed her to assist where time was of the essence for the process.

As she worked, she mentally braced herself for signs of upset or hostility. After all, who was she to come in as lead when they'd been doing the work for months already? If her co-workers did feel that way, they gave no outwards signs; all were welcoming and helped her settle into a groove.

After a few hours, the whole group stopped for a long break. They went downstairs back through the maze of corridors where drinks and food had been laid out in a room for them. Since they weren't permitted to have any liquids, not even water, where they were working, having this room for their comfort was an unexpected perk.

Mac came over to ask her how her morning had been. Although he was in overall charge of the palace conservation and restoration project, during the day he worked as a team leader on painting restoration—available to the other leaders whenever needed but letting them get on with the work at other times.

Priya appreciated his management style. Hopefully, it would give her an opportunity to show what she was capable of—she'd never been leader of such a large team before.

'If your team can spare you for a few minutes, why don't you take a look around the palace and some of the areas we'll be working on next,' he suggested. 'Leo only started outlining the next wall painting so let me have your thoughts on how you think we should proceed with it as soon as you can.'

Priya nodded. 'Of course. Can I wander round on my own or should I find someone from the palace to guide me?'

Mac grinned. 'There are so many people working in the palace at the moment, with everyone getting ready for the gala, we've been allowed to come and go as we need. Believe me, if you stray too close to the royal family's private wing, you'll know.'

'They're not worried we're going to steal their crown jewels then,' Priya joked.

'Most of these rooms are open to the public anyway so anything of worth has been safely stored away. More so now the gala preparations and our restoration work is going on. Just walk around on your own, get a feel of the place. Look at the scope of the work we have ahead. You have the site plan, don't you?'

'I do. I may as well go now. I'll just let my team know.'

Priya spoke to her team then left the room to start exploring the palace. She wandered along corridors with walls covered in huge paintings, showing the island and the palace in different seasons and time periods. It was obvious which paintings had already been restored and she took a vicarious pride in the quality of work her company did. She only hoped she would meet the same thresholds of excellence.

She entered one ballroom where a large wall mosaic of a blue-grey elephant carrying a gold-and-purple howdah glinted in the sunlight coming from the floor-to-ceiling-length arched windows.

Her mother would have loved this. She'd passed away when Priya was eleven, but before then Priya had often gone to visit art galleries and stately homes in Britain with her when she was younger. Her mother had handed down her love of art and architecture. They'd already planned a trip to see the Taj Mahal, Red Fort and the Golden City of Jaisalmer in the summer before Priya started secondary school, which was when her father would be in England for a brief stint before his next posting.

But her mother got sick in Priya's last year of primary school.

Instead of spending time with her vibrant, loving mother, Priya had been sent to boarding school where her father seemed to forget about her existence. She barely saw him after her mother died; she begged to go abroad with him on his postings, but he had always refused. Her only bright moments were holidays she spent with her maternal grandparents who travelled from India to look after her and took her to the places her mum had wanted to show her.

But after a few years, her dadu and didima stopped coming over, so apart from the occasional week with her paternal grandparents who lived in England, she spent holidays at her boarding school.

She never knew why her dadu and didima stopped visiting her. They never replied to her letters or emails or answered her phone calls. After a couple of years she stopped trying. When she lived in India doing fieldwork as part of her master's degree course, she had tried to get in touch again but without success. She briefly considered trying to get in contact now again. Her didima grew up in Adysara; Priya thought she might want to know her granddaughter was working in the palace she used to tell stories about.

Priya grimaced. What was the point of trying to make contact? She would just be inviting further rejection.

Suddenly, the walls of the palace were closing in on her. She was no longer experiencing the awe and joy of exploring. She needed fresh air. She was some distance from the palace exits but she'd passed a ballroom which had open balcony windows.

She retraced her footsteps back to the room.

She walked onto the balcony and breathed in the scent of Adysara, so evocative of India. She tried to find somewhere safe to stand as people were bustling round tidying and decorating. She almost bumped into a platform which was supporting a ladder balanced against a pillar. Luckily she managed to avoid it since someone was perched on the top rung, holding a string of lights.

She lifted her gaze from the man to the top of the pillar. The sun was bright, but she was certain she could see shadows around the edge. Was that…?

'Stop!' she called out. The man tottered slightly on the ladder. Priya held her breath until he regained his balance.

A lady strode up. 'Can I help you? I'm Zivah Chetty, I'm part of the event organiser team at the palace. What is the problem? Who are you?'

Priya introduced herself then explained she'd noticed a hollow relief on the external pillars which hadn't been mentioned in the files.

'Why is it an issue?' Zivah asked.

'It hasn't been assessed yet. We don't know what materials were used. And importantly in this situation, what effect the heat from the lights could have on it. Have these external pillars been assessed for the effects of stringing the lights? I don't see them referenced in my notes.'

'They're pillars.' Her tone was condescending, suggesting Priya was making a fuss over nothing.

'Which are hundreds of years old,' Priya replied.

'If there was a problem your boss and Mr Blake would have pointed it out.'

Priya bit her lip. Zivah Chetty was right. They should have pointed it out. Why wasn't it in the report? Regardless of whether there were actual issues related to the pillars, the hollow relief should have been noted. Perhaps it was a clerical error and the information hadn't been transposed from Leo Blake's notes but she didn't have time to look into it right now. She needed to do an assessment before they went further with the illuminations.

Priya straightened her shoulders, she didn't enjoy arguing with people, but stone art was also an area she specialised in. She did know what she was talking about. As team leader, these were the exact situations she was expected to handle. She had to stand her ground. The potential to damage historical art was too important for her to doubt her abilities.

She needed to get up the ladder.

* * *

'Are my parents in their quarters?' Rohan Varma asked as he strode through the halls of the palace to his suite of rooms.

'The Maharaja is in meetings and the Maharani is visiting the children's hospital with Rajkumari Varasi,' his assistant replied.

'Varasi is here?' he asked, surprised his sister had already arrived on Adysara. 'I presume she and my mother will be out for lunch then?' His assistant nodded. His father wouldn't be stopping for lunch then. Rohan would meet his family for the evening meal, but they had a rule not to discuss business or politics at the dining table. 'Please find me ten minutes to speak to my father this afternoon.'

When he was younger, as soon as he returned home for the holidays from his boarding school, Rohan used to rush to greet his parents wherever they were. His father always stopped what he was doing to spend a few minutes catching up. His father might be the monarch and constitutional head of Adysara, but even when he was in important meetings, he had always made time for Rohan.

When Rohan had children, hopefully within the next five years, he wanted to be the same kind of father—making sure he had time to spend with his family. But before he could become a father, he would need to find a wife. Someone to be the future queen of Adysara. And that was the reason he'd come back from abroad. One of the reasons.

He was thirty-five years old, and fully aware of his duty as the crown prince. Although Adysara hosted a gala week every five years, this year's event would introduce him to eligible woman. Everyone expected him to choose a potential bride.

Rohan had always known this was coming. It was the reason all his previous relationships had necessarily been short-term, and he'd been upfront about it.

Now he was back home, he was ready to do his duty. He was ready to get married.

He went to his rooms for a quick wash and change from his travel clothes into a cotton shirt with a band collar and lightweight wool suit, his usual attire when he was staying in the palace and not having meetings.

Once he felt refreshed, he went to his study. As soon as he sat down, his assistant placed financial reports and policy briefings on his desk. After he'd read through the papers and provided notes he handed the papers over to his assistant. Moments later he could hear the papers being shredded.

Rohan rolled his eyes. Although the palace and the island had fast, effective internet and the palace used its own secure intranet server, his father maintained the tradition of paper reports.

It wasn't the only tradition his father maintained. Rohan was strongly reminded of that fact when he was sitting in front of his father's desk later that afternoon.

They'd spent a pleasant half hour having a quick catch-up on life in general, but his father was in the middle of a busy workday and Rohan wanted to talk about his proposals for Adysara's regeneration.

Rohan loved the history and tradition of Adysara. It was an honour and a privilege to be a member of their royal family. He didn't want to turn his back on it. He wasn't coming back to Adysara with new ideas from his time abroad with the aim of shaking up centuries of tradition. He just wanted to find ways to build on what they were already doing. The country already had a good education and health system but they were constantly losing talented people to emigration because they didn't have the business and market infrastructure to sustain prosperity. But in order for him to create financial stability, he needed his father's formal approval to take his ideas before the government.

It was a slow process. His father was a great believer in the phrase 'if it's not broken, don't fix it.' The problem was his father didn't always admit when something was broken.

Their biggest disagreement was about increasing tourism to the island. Adysara had never been a tourist spot, but its location made it a potentially attractive destination. In Rohan's opinion it could be as popular as the Maldives which had only become a luxury holiday option within the last fifty years.

After a long discussion and using up every ounce of his persuasive ability, Rohan was relieved when his father finally said, 'Fine, son. Look into this regeneration scheme. I'll expect a report from you. I'll put it through the same scrutiny any direct proposal would get. No favours.' He gave Rohan his special smile.

'I would never ask for one. But I have your permission to ask Courthams to do some investigation work?'

'Yes. We can definitely fund the early-stage work from the family finances. But there is one condition.'

Rohan was taken aback. 'There is?'

'Yes. This gala is very important. Not only

for Adysara, but for me and your mother personally. I know you will do your duty.'

'Of course.' It was, always had been and always would be duty above all. It normally went without being said. Surely that wasn't the condition?

No, apparently the condition was for Rohan to discuss the guest list, specifically the female guests, with his father *and* listen to his father's opinions on who could be a good fit for Rohan.

Rohan understood to be a *good fit*, his potential bride would need to offer something which would help with Adysara's growth. Decades ago, one of his ancestor's marriage to a wealthy heiress had enabled the Adysarian royal family to become self-funding—not taking a single coin from the people. Since then, the dynastic marriages had always improved the quality of life for the people of Adysara in some way. At least Rohan didn't have the added requirement to marry someone of royal or noble lineage, although that was an added benefit. Rohan's mother was descended from another Indian royal family, in name only of course, but she still had landed wealth which was used to improve public amenities on the island. Rohan's sister's husband came from a family of tech industrialists which had provided the island with an excellent communication and internet network. Rohan knew he didn't just need to get married—his duty was to make an *advantageous* marriage. Without it, his country could decline even further and even lose its independence. He would never allow that to happen.

'We all hope for a successful outcome from the occasion,' his father said, once they'd gone through the top names under consideration, 'but we would like you to enjoy yourself. It's a time for everyone to have fun. We're not forcing you to make any decisions. Your mother and I just hope you find happiness the way we did.'

At a similar gala forty years ago, his mother had been one of the guests. His father thought they could be compatible together so they'd spent a few months getting to know each other before they agreed to marry. His mother hoped at this gala Rohan would immediately see a woman and fall head first in love, the way she claimed she did with his father.

Although Rohan would never have the temerity to say it to his mother, he believed it was more likely to be lust, not love. Love wasn't something that developed in the space of a few weeks. It grew slowly over time, with shared interests and shared values. It was laughing together, dreaming together, making plans together.

But now, anyone could see the love his parents shared for each other, and their children. And the same was true for his sister and her husband.

Rohan wanted the same kind of relationship with his future wife. He wanted to find someone with mutual interests, someone he could respect, someone he could talk to. Affection or love or whatever they wanted to call it could grow after marriage once they spent time together. He'd seen it happen with his family and friends. It was enough for him.

He'd never been *in love*—he wasn't convinced love existed that way. He'd experienced lust, naturally. He'd had plenty of girlfriends over the years but he was never unhappy when the affair came to an end, as it inevitably did. He was glad of it each time he saw a friend shattered over losing someone they were convinced was the love of their life, only to go through the whole rigmarole again a few months down the line. That kind of *love* was a romantic myth and he wanted nothing to do with it.

Back in his suite of rooms, Rohan walked

over to his windows. The view here, of the manicured grounds with topiary leading to the woods and then his private garden, was very different from his offices in Dubai or Los Angeles where he'd spent most of the past few years. But this place, Adysara, was home. He was happy to be back—for good this time.

One thing he and his father were absolutely on the same page about was that no business, no improvements should spoil the natural beauty of the island. He didn't want to introduce any tourism if it would entail large parts of the natural habitat being destroyed in order to build a sprawling resort. He had ideas to make sure that wouldn't happen.

He made a note to check whether the hoteliers he'd included on his personal guest list for the gala would be able to attend. The companies he'd invited had a reputation for eco-friendly development and sustainability. He hoped the gala events would give him an opportunity to discuss business deals; when he wasn't charming and entertaining his potential brides.

While the guests were staying at the palace for the gala events, Rohan planned to take his potential investors on a tour of the islands which made up Adysara. As well as its location, and the fact there was a functioning monarchy, it was his firm belief the wall paintings and rock-cut sculptures on one of the islands, actually a peninsula off the main island, could be as big a tourist attraction as the caves at Ajanta and Ellora. If he could include those on the tour, it would be a big asset.

He buzzed his assistant. 'Could you arrange for Mr Blake to see me when it's convenient, please.'

A few minutes later, his assistant came through the door, surprising Rohan. That was never a good sign.

'Unfortunately, Mr Blake had to leave. A family emergency I understand,' his assistant explained. 'They organised a replacement immediately—she arrived yesterday.'

Rohan's eyebrows shot up. 'Why is this the first I'm hearing of this?'

'Mr Agrawal was handling it.'

Rohan pressed his lips together. Technically, there was no reason for him to be informed. Govinda Agrawal was the project coordinator after all, but everyone in the palace knew of Rohan's interest in the restoration project. He'd been instrumental in hiring Courtham Conservation Services.

'Who is Mr Blake's replacement?'

His assistant pulled something up on his tablet. 'Priya Sen.'

Rohan frowned. He didn't remember seeing Priya Sen's name on the company website, which meant she couldn't be a recognised expert. The murals and wall carvings were too important to leave in the hands of a junior member of staff.

This was not good.

'Where will I find this Priya Sen?' He was heading to the door as he spoke.

'I can call her to come here.'

Rohan waved away the suggestion. 'No need. I'll go to find her. This can't wait.'

CHAPTER TWO

'PRIYA SEN!'

'Yes,' Priya replied, looking down from her ladder for the person who shouted out to her. There were too many people around for her to pinpoint the speaker. She turned back to the columns.

'Come down here, please!' the voice called out again, the tone of command contradicting the polite words. Whoever this man was, he was used to giving orders.

'Hold on a sec,' Priya called turning back to the column, only to be distracted by the collective gasp from below. They were all looking in the direction of one person.

Even from the height she was at, she could tell the man towered above the people in the ballroom. She watched him stride across to her, making the balcony seem somehow much smaller than it was before. He approached the platform which was balancing her ladder, holding it in an obvious indication he was expecting her to come down. Every instinct screamed at Priya to stay where she was—that going down the ladder and meeting this man was going to have an irrevocable effect on her career—on her life.

She glanced at the other people in the room. All of them had stopped what they were doing and were focused on the interaction between her and the man at the foot of the ladder.

Gulping, she slowly began to descend, taking extra care with each step she didn't miss her footing. With all eyes trained on her, the last thing she wanted was to fall in a heap.

She hated being the centre of attention.

Once she finally reached the ground, she patted down her overalls then looked up at the man waiting for her.

And time stopped.

He was a walking work of art; his hair was black, so black the sunlight cast a blue sheen across it, his cheekbones were sharp as if they'd been chiselled from marble, his jaw strong and stubborn, impatient. And his deep, dark brown eyes didn't hide his annoyance.

'Priya Sen,' the man said, his voice rippling over her body.

She blinked, still not quite believing the image of beauty before her was real.

'You are Priya Sen, are you not. I hear you've taken over from Leo Blake.'

'Priya. Yes, yes that's my name. Priya. And I've replaced Leo.' Priya hoped she'd managed a genuine-looking smile but the stretch in her cheeks suggested otherwise. 'Oh, are you the palace coordinator? I've been looking forward to meeting you, Mr Agrawal.' She held out her hand. The man simply stared at it. Priya grimaced. So much for making a good impression. She immediately drew her hand back, then put both her palms together, touching her forehead with her fingers.

The man inclined his head.

'I'm not Mr Agrawal,' he said. 'I'm Rohan Varma.'

'Varma?' Priya tilted her head. It was the surname of the royal family. It wasn't a unique surname so it probably wasn't that much of a coincidence he also had the same one. But the expectant look he was giving her, put together with the deferential silence of the other people nearby who were still watching their exchange, gave her pause for thought.

Of course she'd done an internet search of Adysara and its royal family. She'd seen pictures of them. But the truth was she didn't have a great memory for faces and her focus had been on the heritage of the place, not the people.

She had to admit it was possible she was standing in front of a member of the royal family of Adysara. She stood immobilised like a deer caught in the headlights. Would it be rude to ask him if he were royalty? Wasn't it something she should be expected to know?

'Yuvaraja-sahib,' Zivah Chetty said. 'How can I assist you?'

Priya gulped. Zivah had addressed him as the prince, no not just the prince, the crown prince. There was now no possible doubt the man in front of her was part of the royal family. Not Mr Agrawal, the project coordinator. Not even Mr Agrawal's manager. But the crown prince. And she'd told him to hold on.

Was it too late for her to dip into a curtsey— no, the etiquette guide, which the team had been given before they started working, said curtseying was only necessary if she was a citizen of Adysara.

She slowly became aware the prince and Zivah were looking at her expectantly. While her mind had been filtering thoughts about etiquette and royal families, she'd obviously missed the conversation.

She inwardly berated herself. Being singled out by the prince wasn't a good sign. If there was anyone she wanted to make a good impression on it would be Rohan Varma. She'd been told the crown prince took a personal interest in the conservation work. She could only hope she could salvage the situation. There was no way she would be able to convince Mac she was the right person to keep leading the project if she couldn't impress the prince.

She opened her mouth, but the only thing which came out was a choked sound. She took a calming breath. She couldn't let her nerves and doubts get the better of her. Not now. This was too important for her future.

'Perhaps we could talk, Ms Sen,' the prince said.

'Of course, Yuvaraja-sahib,' Priya replied, using the same form of address Zivah had, assuming she must know the correct designation. She walked behind him as he led her out of the ballroom.

All her colleagues had talked about how invested the prince was, but from what they said, she'd been under the impression he wasn't on this island.

If she thought about it, she supposed it made sense he would return well before the gala. In the few hours she'd been on the island, she'd already heard the rumour this particular event was for him to find a bride. She wasn't sure whether she really believed that—it sounded too much like a fairy tale—but she was aware the Adysara royal family only hosted the lavish gala festivities every five years.

The prince led her towards an empty reception room. Once inside he closed the door and turned to her. She didn't have to be an empath to recognise the restrained anger in the tight lines of his jaw.

She had no idea what she could have done to cause his reaction. But if he didn't want her as project lead her professional dreams were over before they'd even got started.

'What were you doing hanging lights on the pillars?' he bit out at her. 'I was told you've taken over from Leo Blake as team lead on the wall restorations. I don't think decorating for the party is an objective of the role. If you're going to stay here, I expect you to do your job.'

Priya's mouth fell open. She blinked trying to understand what he was talking about. Hanging lights?

'I—I wasn't,' was all she could say.

His mouth tightened, making Priya gulp. Her denial made him angrier.

'You weren't on the ladder just now.' He quirked an eyebrow.

'Yes, of course, but I—'

'You weren't hanging the lights?'

'No!' Priya closed her eyes trying to remember what had happened to the string of the lights the person had been about to attach to the pillar before she stopped him. She didn't recall him bringing them down with him. He must have left the lights at the top of the ladder, she just hadn't noticed.

She supposed from the ground, it could look like she was helping with decorations rather than working. She needed to set the story straight.

'I know it may have looked like I was attaching the lights, but I wasn't.' She held her hand up when he opened his mouth to speak. 'I stopped someone because I needed to examine the pillar.' It was only when she noticed the startled expression on his face that she realised by her hand gesture she'd effectively told the prince to shut up.

Mortification didn't begin to describe the sudden heat in her cheeks contrasting with the feeling of cold dread rushing through her body.

Waiting for him to chastise her for her impertinence, she raised her eyebrows when instead he asked, 'Why did you need to examine the pillar?'

'I thought I'd seen an intaglio in the pillar. I didn't see anything about them in the reports. I needed to do an examination before they could be damaged by the lights or heat.'

'An intaglio in the pillars?'

'Yes. A hollow relief. It's a—'

'I know what a relief is.'

She gave a brief nod of acknowledgement. 'I wasn't one hundred percent sure from the ground. And I couldn't see anything on other pillars. So I had to go up on the platform to investigate.'

'You thought there was a relief on one pillar of the balcony nobody has noticed before?'

Priya looked at her feet. He made it sound like she was being ridiculous. 'I was right. There was something. There was no mention of it before—probably because our restoration project was asked to concentrate on the internal rooms. We should have checked all the areas which are going to be decorated. The artwork in this palace is so amazing, it's not a surprise to find there are gems hidden in unexpected places.'

The prince was quiet for a few moments. Then he nodded his head. 'So you think there could be other places in the palace with similar reliefs or other artwork?'

Priya nodded. 'We should definitely check any areas which are being decorated, whether or not a main event is taking place there. Particularly outside.'

There was a knock at the door. Someone Priya didn't recognise popped his head in.

'Yuvaraja-sahib,' the man said, 'it's time for your call.'

The prince glanced at his watch. 'We can discuss this later. Come to my study after dinner. Eight thirty.'

He walked away without giving her a backward glance.

Priya took a couple of deep breaths. At least she wasn't fired. It sounded like he accepted she had a genuine reason to be on the ladder. It was probably as close to an apology as she was going to get for being accused of decorating rather than doing her job.

So on the one hand, she'd shown competence in her field. On the other hand, she'd told the crown prince of Adysara to hold on and then stopped him when he tried to speak. Priya closed her eyes tightly. If her actions had caused her to lose this position, she would only have herself to blame. No wonder Mac hadn't picked her for the initial team.

Suddenly, the thought occurred to her she had no idea where the prince's study was. She mentally shrugged. She was sure someone in the group would be able to direct her. Speaking of which, she'd been away from the work much longer than she planned. She couldn't risk her team thinking she was unreliable and not pulling her weight, not after all her mistakes with the prince.

She headed back to join them.

Rohan tried to concentrate on the policy document in front of him. He glanced at his watch. Priya Sen was five minutes late. He couldn't remember the last time someone kept him waiting. Well, apart from this morning. But somehow he didn't think Priya was doing it intentionally.

Perhaps it was arrogance on his part but he was so used to being treated with respect, almost reverence, whenever he was at home, he hadn't anticipated Priya wouldn't know he was the crown prince. She'd been polite but in no way deferential.

It was a relief nobody could see his face as he watched Priya come down from the platform. He'd never thought overalls were a particularly alluring item of clothing until he'd been entranced by Priya's curvaceous figure descending towards him. He'd been eager to see her face, and when she finally did look at him, something intense flared in him.

She was stunning. There was no better word to describe her.

His physical reaction to her was natural. But inappropriate. He was the crown prince, with a duty to choose a bride within the next few months; he couldn't indulge in a brief sexual fling. And even if it wasn't the case, his interest in Priya had to remain professional.

There could only be business between them.

The intercom announced Priya was in the waiting area. Briefly tempted to keep her waiting for a while, he curtailed the immature impulse and signalled his assistant to let her in.

She was red-faced and panting. Had she taken a shower before this meeting or was her hair damp with sweat? Whichever it was, it didn't detract from her innate beauty.

Rohan pressed his lips together, reminding himself he had no business thinking of the way Priya looked.

'I'm so sorry,' she gasped out. 'I got lost and nobody would tell me how to get here for security reasons.'

Rohan frowned. 'Didn't Hoshik meet you?'

he asked, referring to a member of his personal staff.

Priya gave a small self-deprecating laugh. 'In the end yes. But I didn't know you were sending someone to fetch me. I didn't want to be late for our meeting so I set off before Hoshik arrived at our building. In the end I decided to return to our quarters and there he was. I am so sorry.'

Rohan quashed a laugh. She looked nervous and frazzled—he doubted she'd see the humour in the situation. Did she really think she could wander around the palace and be directed to his suite simply by asking people? He only hoped her job portfolio was accurate and her expertise in stone-cut art was better than her common sense.

'Can I get you a drink?' he asked, waiting for her to get her breath.

'No!' She looked horrified at the suggestion. Then she closed her eyes, clearly embarrassed. 'Oh, you mean get someone to get me a drink. No, thank you.'

Rohan rolled his eyes. He couldn't really take offence at the implication he couldn't get his own drinks—he didn't have staff or workers when he lived in the States and he had the bare minimum staff in Dubai—but unfortunately, the reality was in the palace he rarely lifted a finger for himself and was in fact going to ask his assistant to fetch her drink, if she asked for anything other than spirits he had in his study.

She perched primly at the edge of her seat, trying to maintain eye contact with him, but often looking down at her lap, whether out of nerves or deference to his royal status he wasn't sure.

He glanced at the folder on his desk. From what he'd read, she had no need to be nervous about her qualifications and ability to take on the project lead role.

'I had a chance to look through your portfolio,' he began, 'it's impressive.'

'Thank you,' she replied, her voice rising at the end, as if she was surprised by his comment. Didn't she know how strong her professional background was?

'You have a specific qualification in wall conservation. Why weren't you part of the project to begin with?'

'I don't know. I wasn't part of the decision-making process.'

He narrowed his eyes. She was clearly uncomfortable by his question. He suspected she had hoped she would be part of the group as well.

'I'm very happy to be a member of the team

now. And of course, my manager has said we'd be happy to take a look at any other projects you have in mind while we're here.' She reached into her bag for a notebook.

He gave a brief nod, pleased she'd brought the conversation directly to the business at hand.

When they had met earlier on the balcony, he'd got the impression she was unsure of her position and role. It made him worry she wasn't the right person to take over the project. But a lot of it was due to her soft features and her delicate round face, which made her look far too young to be leading a project.

He huffed. What Priya looked like was irrelevant. He was only interested in her talents at preservation.

'I don't know how much you know about Adysara.'

'A little.'

'We're actually an archipelago of ten islands, although only four are currently inhabited. Technically those four islands could be considered peninsulas, but access is tricky by land. Although a lot of people assume we're part of India, we're actually self-governing and self-financing.'

She nodded her head. So she had done her research.

'We have good trading relationships with South Asia and North Africa, but if we are to be sustainable in the long term, we need to look at bringing in other revenue streams.'

She furrowed her brow, wrinkling her nose in a manner he found delightful. He averted his gaze so he could concentrate properly.

'We have a summer palace, which we don't use any more on one of the islands. It could be turned into a luxury resort island, but I believe cultural heritage also attracts tourists. To that end, there are at least six murals on some of the smaller islands which I think could be worthy of displaying as tourist attractions. But the major thing is on what we call Adysarina Island which has rock-cut architecture in caves. I want to do an exploratory project on whether we can open those caves up to visitors and perhaps get some tourist revenue.'

'I'm not the team expert on restoration matters.'

'I know.' He waved her portfolio briefly. 'Obviously I would like the wall paintings and cave art to be restored. But before that can be done, the first priority—'

'The first priority is to do a survey to assess the condition and causes of any deterioration.' She flashed a bright, but brief, smile at him.

'Precisely.' He sensed she approved of his priorities.

'Fantastic.' She clapped her hands together. 'I can do a visual inspection with the equipment I have on the island. When can I begin the evaluation?'

'I will arrange for you to tour the islands, beginning with the murals. Once you've inspected those, you can look at the caves. It probably isn't feasible to attract tourists with merely the caves to entice them.'

Priya gave a one-shoulder shrug. 'Apparently Ajanta and Ellora do quite well.'

His lips quirked. 'Have you visited those caves?'

'No. I've been to the Elephanta Caves. Actually my visit there started my interest in heritage conservation.'

'I noticed you were a science major at university.'

She smiled. 'That's what my bachelor's degree is in, yes. But then I visited the Elephanta Caves, saw the dvarapalas and the linga shrine and knew I needed to work in this field. It was a big gamble to change direction from the science doctorate I was sure I would be taking, particularly since I'm not artistic and had no real knowledge of art.' She paused then cleared her throat, as if suddenly aware she was sharing unnecessary personal information. 'Do you have any photographs or schematics for the murals and caves? What's their current preservation situation?'

'We already had architects and engineers appraise the areas. I'll make sure you have their reports.'

She was sitting forward now, showing her eagerness to find out more about the project, her finger tapping against her mouth drawing his gaze to the lush fullness of her lips.

He needed to stop this. Rohan stood up and walked towards a bureau which contained a drinks cabinet. He poured himself a Scotch, belatedly turning to offer Priya something, which she refused. He worked with many beautiful women, all the time. He never let their attractiveness distract him.

Perhaps it was the circumstances, which was causing this unusual reaction rather than Priya Sen herself. He was back home to find a potential bride. Someone he could spend his life with. Perhaps he was inadvertently assessing people he met—women he met—as future spouses. Which immediately knocked Priya out of contention. She would never be a suitable bride for him.

He had to remain professional. He might not be her direct employer, but his family were, and if they worked on the cave project together he would certainly be thought of as a client.

CHAPTER THREE

TWO DAYS LATER, Priya waited at the front doors of the palace for a car to be brought round. It was only February, which she'd read was the coldest, driest month on the island, but the sun hadn't received the message and was already threatening a scorcher. It was going to be a long, hot day.

Luckily, a palace worker had already handed her a cool bag with bottled water for her day out.

When the Jeep came into view, a tall, well-built man came to stand next to her. She gave him a small smile, but his face remained impassive. She tried asking him who he was but he gave no indication he could understand her English. She didn't know Adsahi, the native language of Adysara, so she tried in Hindi, one of Adysara's national languages, but he still didn't reply.

She shrugged. Hindi wasn't her family's

regional language, but she'd picked up some
words and phrases growing up, and it had
improved when she was doing fieldwork in
India as part of her master's. Apparently not
well enough to be understood by the man next
to her though.

A worker ran out from a small side building holding a long pole with a mirror on the
end, which he handed to the man. When the
Jeep came to a halt, the silent man walked
round the vehicle, using the mirror to look
under it. He gave a small nod to someone in
the doorway.

Priya widened her eyes. Was he some kind
of palace security? There had been so much
freedom in moving around the palace and its
grounds, she almost forget it was actually the
home of the royal family.

The man took Priya's bags of equipment
to load in the boot. Then he held one of the
doors open for Priya so she got in the car. It
was still early, but the heat made the temper-
ature in the car uncomfortable. She reached
into her bag to pull out a bottle of water and
a cloth to wipe her face.

As she was taking a sip, a shadow to her
side indicated someone was getting in. She
pasted a bright smile on her face, wishing
the first impression she would be making on

Mr Agrawal wasn't with sweat pouring down her face.

But that would have been better than making the same bad impression on Prince Rohan, who had actually got into the car.

She wasn't usually vain, so why should it bother her she was never looking her best when they met? Her concern must be she wasn't looking professional. Particularly when compared to the effortlessly cool and poised man sitting next to her.

After a brief nod of acknowledgement he started speaking to the two men in the front seats. She took the chance to examine him, unobserved.

A bold, straight nose. His full, surprisingly sensuous lips prominent despite the shadow of his beard. Again, she imagined his rigid profile immortalised in stone.

Maybe it already had been. Was there a bust, or a full-length statue of him somewhere in the palace grounds? She would love to see it.

'Everything all right?' his voice interrupted her musings.

'Yes. Fine.' She smiled as brightly, but professionally as she could.

'Shall we go then?'

'Aren't we waiting for Mr Agrawal?'

'He's busy in the palace. I can show you the relevant murals.'

Wasn't the prince busy? He was heir to the throne. Surely he shouldn't be spending his time showing her around the island. From their conversation a couple of evenings ago, she could understand how important the regeneration project was to him, but she didn't want to be a burden—she could inspect the murals on her own.

'Yuvaraja-sahib—'

'You can call me Rohan.'

'Oh, I don't think I could,' she replied without thinking. 'I'm not sure it's appropriate.'

He took a slow breath, the kind she knew people took when they were gathering their patience.

'We're going to be working together for a while over the next few days.' He spoke slowly. 'I don't want to always be addressed as the prince. It's not necessary. It's also not safe to draw attention to my royal status when we're out in public. I don't want everyone to know I'm outside the palace. And luckily, when people don't expect to see me they can't be sure I am the prince, as I have no doubt you can understand.'

She knew he was making a dig about her failure to recognise him at their first meeting, but his tone didn't sound irritated—it sounded humorous.

'I also have this baseball cap,' he added, pulling one out of his pocket and placing it on his head. 'No one expects the prince to wear this.'

Priya laughed. She reached out and adjusted the cap to sit better. The cap did nothing to disguise his handsome features, but it made him look more down to earth—not so out of reach. She blinked then hastily withdrew her hand before turning her head to look out of the window.

Why had she done that? He *was* out of reach, she reminded herself. He was royalty. She didn't understand why she was having such an unusual reaction to him. He was an attractive man. Maybe she was experiencing what her friends felt about their celebrity crushes. That must be it—her shallow breath and accelerated heartbeat must be because she was in the presence of someone famous.

Nothing to worry about—her career was the only thing important to her and it didn't allow her room for distractions. Finding the crown prince attractive was safe in a way, because he was so far out of her league he would never be interested in someone like her and nothing could come from this harmless crush.

But if he wanted to be treated as a client, she could treat him as one. And she was often asked to call her clients by their first names.

She turned back to him. 'Very well. If you insist, Rohan,' she replied, emphasising his name.

'I do. Now we're going to be travelling down some very rocky and uneven paths, which is why we're taking the Jeep. If we do open this area as a tourist attraction, naturally we will improve the infrastructure, but I thought I should warn you. It could be bumpy.'

'I'm sure I'll be fine,' she replied. 'I'm made of hardy stock.'

He made a choking sound but didn't say anything. After a minute, he picked up the electronic tablet which was on his lap. 'Do you mind if I do some work?' he asked, but without waiting for a reply he started scrolling on it.

Priya turned to look out the window again. This was her first chance to get a good look at the island.

The road wound through a hill, and the altitude allowed Priya a view of the forests, rows of houses of different sizes constructed from stone or red bricks with flat rooves giving views over the beaches edging the seemingly endless ocean waters. She sighed, completely at peace.

As the Jeep continued to ascend, she began to experience the roughness of the terrain. Only a few bumps, but she braced one hand against the side of the car and checked the security of her seat belt with the other. More jostling, faster and harder now. She struggled to remain seated until they went over a large hump which flung her off her seat and across the car. She would have landed on the floor at Rohan's feet but strong arms caught her before she fell.

Without missing a beat, he helped her sit upright and reached round her to put her seat belt back on.

He gave an instruction to the driver, who slowed down significantly before coming to a stop at a safe part of the road.

The bodyguard came round to hold the door open for her. After she exited, he bent inside and she could see him fiddle with the seat belt. Rohan, the bodyguard and the driver had a quick discussion—plenty of hand gestures and shaking heads but Priya had no idea what they were talking about.

Rohan came over to her. 'We can't find anything wrong with the seat belt. It doesn't look like sabotage, but we will get our mechanics to look at the car when we return to the palace. Would you like to return now? You should be safe if you move to the middle seat. Alternatively you can swap places with Taj,' he said, referring to his bodyguard.

Priya was still trying to process the implication behind Rohan's use of the word *sabotage*.

'Priya,' Rohan's voice penetrated her thoughts. 'Do you want to return to the palace?'

'No, please. We've come all this way. There's no reason to delay this.'

'Are you sure?'

'Yes. I told you. Hardy—'

'Hardy stock. I remember.' The briefest hint of a smiled played on Rohan's lips, but it was enough to send Priya's pulse soaring.

She might be suffering a small celebrity crush, but Priya wasn't sure she really needed the added temptation of sitting next to Rohan for the rest of the journey. She glanced at Taj, standing where he could survey the land and protect Rohan at a moment's notice. There must have been a safety and security reason for the bodyguard to be sitting in the front seat to begin with. She wasn't going to do anything which would jeopardise the prince's safety.

She took the seat in the middle. Taj double-checked her seat belt and they continued the journey. Priya hyperfocused on the report on the murals Rohan had sent her, trying desperately to ignore the warmth from the body next to her and the shivers which ran up her spine at every unintentional contact.

She didn't think she'd ever been as relieved for a journey to be over when Rohan finally said, 'We're here.'

Priya got out of the car and walked round to join Rohan as he led her to an old, crumbling, stone building which was probably used as a hunting lodge or dowager's home in the past.

The lodge had been built into the side of a hill so when she entered through a large arch, it was onto a first-floor walkway which overlooked a courtyard, which once had a large pond. She slowly followed Rohan's gaze to one side.

'Oh, my,' was all she could manage as she began taking in the centuries-old wall painting depicting a group of women in dance poses although only their hands and faces were visible since the mural was the length of the two floors.

'How do we get down there?' She turned to ask Rohan. She started going round the walkway looking for steps that would take them downstairs, then came back to where they entered. 'Oh, I should get my equipment out of the car first.' She craned her neck to glimpse the top of the mural. 'This is simply breathtaking in person, Rohan. I can't believe something like this exists,' she said turning her gaze to his.

He gave her a warm, genuine smile. And for a moment she wasn't sure the mural was actually the most breathtaking thing she'd seen that morning.

'Come on, let's go,' Rohan said, so Priya hurried to collect her things.

Rohan stood at a distance from the wall. He never stopped marvelling at the artistry that went into this mural in front of him. There were no records detailing when the work was created—it wasn't unusual, written records had been rare on the island until the nineteenth century. It wasn't clear whether someone, possibly the royal family at the time, had commissioned the work or whether this was someone's labour of love. But the land it was on belonged to the royal family now and he was its willing caretaker.

'The problem with these murals is they weren't created with longevity in mind,' Priya said as she took moisture measurements and light readings. 'A lot of them were simply ostentatious ways to show how wealthy the person who commissioned the work was. And of course, they didn't have the chemicals and equipment we have today. But why am I telling you things you already know.'

'It's incredible how they created the colours at the time.'

Priya shrugged. 'Well over time the colours became easier to mix. You can see the difference as we come down the painting.'

Rohan frowned. 'What do you mean?'

'This mural isn't one cohesive body of work. You can see the slight changes where different artists took over.' She indicated some areas.

He wasn't an artist and hadn't studied art. To his untrained eye, everything looked the same.

'The bottom has been surprisingly well preserved, which is unusual since I would estimate this was the oldest part. I would say fourteen hundreds, but you would need Mac to test and verify. You'll also need an architectural and engineering report on the structural integrity of the building itself before any tourists come. It would help to have their analysis before we begin working here.' She went back to the mural, happily answering his questions as she worked.

'This is incredible. There are signs of early preservation attempts to some areas. None of our modern methods, but they are definitely using techniques from this century. Who has been maintaining this area?' Priya asked. 'Can I speak to them?'

'All the murals and the stonework you'll see later have been maintained by Mr Agrawal's team. We haven't had experts in, before now. Once these murals were discovered, a couple of hundred years ago, the family closed off public access as a way of conserving them. The palace records show they are open to the public for limited times of the year. But there isn't much interest. Once the islanders have seen the mural, not many come on return visits.'

'I can understand the desire to show this to the world. I saw in the reports you gave me these works are not considered to be within the areas of the Archaeological Society of India, but did you ask them to send someone to inspect it?'

'No.' He grimaced. 'My father and grandfather have never had much interest in opening this area to tourists so there was no need to consider conservation and preservation from such a perspective.'

'I don't need to tell you about all the extra

considerations that need to be taken into account when exposing this kind of work to hundreds of people. At the same time it would be so sad to keep something like this hidden from the world.'

'It's not just because of the art, my father doesn't want to encourage tourism.' Now why had he admitted that to her? It was a personal issue.

She paused what she was doing and tilted her head, waiting for him to say more.

He supposed it wasn't really personal—she already knew about his regeneration plans and the majority of the administration knew he wanted to actively explore increasing tourism to the island. He needed to be honest with Priya and let her know all the work she would be putting into the murals could never come to fruition. But how much detail was it necessary to tell her?

He briefly outlined the issues. As he spoke, he felt a deep sorrow he was at odds with his father. There was so much potential in this plan. But his family was more important.

He sometimes considered giving up on his proposal for regeneration in order to keep the peace despite being convinced it would reap benefits for Adysara's economic growth in the long run. He'd always gone along with what his family wanted in the past—and had been happy to. It was a privilege to be part of the royal family so he willingly carried out his responsibilities. He never wanted to disappoint his parents or have them worry he wasn't doing his duty.

'I understand,' she replied, breaking into his thoughts. 'I think it's important to look at conserving these murals, and if the stone-cut artwork in the caves is anything like this, it will be vitally important. I can prepare a couple of proposals since obviously if you don't have tourists you won't have the same concerns about footfall, lighting, et cetera.'

'Sounds good.'

She turned back to the mural. 'It sounds like being in a royal family is like working in a family business.'

'It's very much like that, yes.'

The horrified expression on her face as she looked over her shoulder at him made it clear she hadn't meant to make her comment out loud. He liked the way she spoke to him as any other client. Not even a client, a friend?

After spending so much time living in different countries where nobody knew about his royal status it took him some time to get used to the deferential, unearned respect people who knew he was a prince tended to treat him with.

'I did run a couple of businesses in Los Angeles and Dubai. I've spent most of my time travelling between the three places. It was good to create something without family expectations, although I can't pretend I wasn't hugely advantaged by the financial situation. From what you mentioned at our meeting the other night, it sounds like you aren't following in the family footsteps by doing this line of work.'

Her lips thinned. That was unusual. Why would the mention of her family cause her reaction?

'No. My father is in the diplomatic service. He has postings around the world.'

'What a great opportunity for you to explore different countries.'

She gave a toneless laugh. 'Hardly. I never get to see him.'

Her voice was so quiet at her last sentence, he almost missed it.

'You don't see your father?' Rohan couldn't imagine not having a close relationship with his parents. They may have been busy with their royal duties, or away in different countries, but they always made time to chat, by video if necessary.

Priya shrugged. 'Like I said, he works away.'

'But you said postings. Doesn't he spend time with you in England?'

'No. He goes from one foreign posting to another. When I was younger, before my mum died, we used to travel with him, but afterwards I went to boarding school. He's deputy head of mission now. I think he would love to be an ambassador one day, but it hasn't happened yet.'

He could tell she was trying to speak in a matter-of-fact tone, but was he sensing some underlying sadness? No, he didn't know her well enough to understand the nuances of her conversations.

'Was your boarding school in England? Which one? I went to boarding school in England when I was fifteen to study for my GCSEs.'

She told him which one. He knew it well. His family had considered it an option for him.

'How come you went to England for your GCSEs?' she asked.

'I went to different boarding schools around the world. Until the age of eleven I went to a school in North India. Afterwards I spent a few years in the States, Europe and Africa.'

'Oh, God, that's awful. I know how miserable it can be.'

'What? No?' He'd loved being at boarding school. It had been the perfect environment for him. He made friendships easily so moving to a new school was never a problem for him. It sounded like Priya had a very different experience. Perhaps because, despite being in a different country, he was constantly in touch with his family and home. They were a strong presence in his life even when they weren't physically with him.

There was something about Priya that prevented him from feeling pity. Compassion, definitely. But Priya wasn't giving the impression she felt sorry for herself.

'You mentioned you discovered your love of conservation after you visited the Elephanta Caves. Who took you?' he asked.

'My grandparents. My mum's parents. It was the last time I saw them.'

This time he definitely heard an underlying sadness.

'I'm sorry for your loss.'

'Oh, I don't know if they're dead. They just…' She broke off and then shook her head. 'It doesn't matter.' She walked over to a corner of the wall. 'Look at this. There's some damage here but I think the tabla player and the flautist have their eyes covered. I think this fresco is showing palace dancers. Do you know whether this building was used for a king's courtesans?'

It was a good thing Priya had refocused their attention on the mural. On the project. He had started out making polite conversation, trying to put her at ease. But her background piqued his interest.

Not to mention the strong urge he had to take her into his arms and comfort her for her unhappiness at boarding school; for the loss of her mum, and her maternal grandparents; and her father though it sounded like he was still alive.

There was still a lot he wanted to unpack but, despite some of the openness in her sharing some of her childhood experiences, she had immediately erected a barrier between them.

And that was a good thing.

CHAPTER FOUR

PRIYA RUSHED THROUGH her lunch then had a quick meeting with her team, making sure everyone was happy with what they were doing that afternoon, before heading outside to the waiting car ready to visit the next mural. After seeing the first mural three days before, she had been impatient to see Adysara's other hidden treasures but had determined, since she was still new to the team, it would be best if she spent at least two days working on the palace murals between each site visit.

The car set off as soon as Priya had settled in. She sank back into the seat—Rohan wasn't coming with her. What had she expected? A prince would be her tour guide every day? But he was so excited when he showed her the mural the previous time, she'd secretly been hoping he'd accompany her again.

Perhaps it was for the best. She still couldn't

believe she'd told him about her father. She never talked about him with anyone.

After their rather rocky start, Rohan had made her feel at ease to the extent she kept forgetting he was a prince. In fact she sometimes forgot he was a potential client, speaking to him as a colleague who shared her love of the artistry they were viewing. He didn't seem to mind. Even encouraged her to share her stories.

It had been nice to talk to someone about the work. She regularly worked as part of a team, but she found it hard to make small talk as most of the other team members did. They usually did scoping work in a small group, but since this wasn't something previously scheduled and the team had deadlines to meet for the conservation and restoration work in the palace, Mac suggested she could complete the scoping on her own. He sounded pleased with the potential of the future project and was happy for her to take whatever time she needed to prepare the report so their company would, hopefully, get the contract.

If they did get the job, it would be big. And she would honestly achieve one of her biggest goals if she could persuade Mac she should lead the project—not just one of the teams but the entire project. She couldn't imagine anything more incredible or rewarding than to be responsible for not only preserving the glory of the island's murals and sculptures, but also doing it in a way that would potentially allow the glory to be seen by others, rather than hidden from sight for their protection. She had the qualifications and experience. Would that be enough? Perhaps she should broach the topic with Mac.

Not yet—she needed to prove her value to the team before she could expect anyone to think of her as capable of fulfilling the role. She also didn't want to step out of place. If Leo Blake returned and wanted to lead the work, then she probably wouldn't be considered. What would be the point of submitting an expression of interest if Leo wanted it? When the palace contract had originally come up she'd wanted to express her interest, but then Leo told her he was applying for the stone conservation lead so she'd dropped the idea. Why risk being turned down?

The car came to a halt outside a small woodland area. The driver helped her out of the car and then led her down a path until they came to a clearing where a mural depicting the trees and bushes they had just passed had been painted onto the stone side of a small cliff. Unfortunately, the birds, brightly painted in blues and golds, didn't have real life counterparts she could see.

She sighed at the beauty in front of her, sending up a wish even if she wasn't good enough to lead it, she would still get the chance to be part of this work.

She'd been conducting her examination for a while, when she heard someone clear their throat behind her. She glanced at the time and realised she'd become so absorbed in what she was doing, a few hours had passed. Turning around she expected to see the driver telling her it was time to return. Her heart skipped a beat when she saw who it actually was.

'Rohan,' she exclaimed in delight. 'I didn't know you were coming.'

He gave her a puzzled look. Had she been too informal? She was always getting this protocol wrong. She didn't know what the protocol was. The previous time he'd invited her to call him Rohan, but today he looked surprised by her use of his first name. Was she expected to wait for his permission to use his name each time?

He was a client and a prince. A prince and a client. Not a friend.

'It's another masterpiece,' she said, turning to the mural after he still hadn't said anything.

'Incredible. Can you imagine having this much talent. I couldn't stop thinking about the craftsmanship after I first saw them when I was still young. I knew they were special even though I haven't studied art.'

'Well neither have I,' Priya replied, with a slight laugh.

'Oh, yes. I remember. You did a science bachelor's.'

'That's right. Natural sciences.'

'Your boarding school has a reputation for being a science school. Was that why you studied science rather than art or art history?'

She giggled. 'No. I didn't study art because I can't draw. It's part of the reason I went into the conservation and preservation side, not restoration.'

'No family expectation you'd be a doctor then?' he asked. She recognised the stereotype immediately.

'No. No doctors in my family. How about you? No pressure to be a doctor for you?'

His lips quirked and she didn't understand why he was looking at her like she'd just said the funniest thing he'd ever heard.

'What?' she asked.

'No. No doctor for me.' He cleared his throat. 'Actually the family expectation is I will be... um...king.'

Priya didn't know how it was possible for her body to run hot with embarrassment and at the same time freeze with mortification.

She held her hands to her mouth. 'Of course. Of course you're going to be king. You're the prince.' She covered her mouth with her fingertips then fluttered them against her lips as she said, 'But of course you know that.' She closed her eyes as if not being able to see meant she was the one who would disappear. Could she say anything more ridiculous?

'Priya.' Rohan's voice was gentle. 'Priya, it's all right. There's nothing wrong with forgetting I'm a prince. I try to do it all the time.'

She opened her eyes quickly. 'What? Why?'

'My parents wanted us, my sister and me, to live as normal a life as we could for as long as we could. My mother wasn't brought up as royalty, despite being descended from one of the royal families in India, and she didn't want our position to shape us negatively. Whenever I'm outside this country, I live as Rohan Varma. Ordinary citizen. It's an adjustment to be back on the island, back in the palace where I'm Rohan Varma, Yuvaraja, and I have a bodyguard and people to make my food and tidy my clothes away.'

'But you don't mind it.' She could hear in his voice he wasn't complaining.

'Not at all. It's my duty. It's what I was born to do. The first time I returned after living on my own and fending for myself, I thought I didn't need all the staff and asked to make a reduction. But the palace is a large employer for the island. If I didn't have those people carry out tasks they've been doing for years, even though I can do them myself, then they become unemployed and I wasn't going to be responsible for that. So if I have someone hang my clothes then it's a privilege. Although I did draw the line at someone spreading toothpaste on my brush.'

Priya's celebrity crush just got a whole lot bigger. What a considerate person he was.

'Anyway,' he continued, 'I'm grateful my parents gave me the opportunity. I appreciate I got the chance to get to make friends as me, as the person I am.'

It would be hard not to want to be friends with Rohan—but he was her client not her friend. She had to drill it into her brain somehow and get her body to pay attention.

'I can see how it would be special,' she said, trying to adopt a measured tone. 'Will your friends be coming to your gala?'

'I'm expecting some close friends. Friends I was close enough to reveal my royal status to. I hope some friends I had at boarding school will be able to come too. We've kept in touch over the years although we haven't had the chance to meet up as much as we wanted to.'

Priya gave a tight smile and then turned back to the mural. She hadn't made any close friends when she was at boarding school. She didn't blame her fellow classmates. She didn't accept the few invitations she did receive, knowing she could never return the hospitality. After a while people stopped asking her. She'd been utterly miserable and probably didn't give anyone the impression she wanted friends.

It was strange how she and Rohan had similar backgrounds, but from what she could gather, he'd been extremely happy growing up—even loving his boarding school experience.

For her, boarding school had been a constant reminder of how her dad didn't want her with him. He'd definitely kept her out of sight and out of mind.

She tried to imagine how her father would react if he knew she was working in the palace, on first name terms with a crown prince. She sighed. The truth was she didn't know her father at all and had no idea whether he would be proud of her. She never received a response to her message telling him she'd completed her master's with distinction or when she told him she'd got the job with the world-renowned Courtham Conservation Services. And her attempts to keep in contact since then had been brief to say the least.

There was no point thinking about her father or her family. Her priority was to get the murals in the palace completed, and hopefully do a good enough job she would be considered for the preservation work on these murals.

'Have you seen this?' Rohan said, beckoning her over to something painted on the ground.

'I've never been able to work out what this is,' he said. She grinned as he ran through all the ideas he'd had—his excitement clear. She made a feeble joke suggestion for what the damaged area showed, but his laugh was hearty, the sound sending tingles along her spine.

Rohan was probably taught how to be charming and entertaining at the same time he had learned his alphabet but Priya recognised these few hours in his company were some of the happiest she'd felt in a long time.

She had to keep her attraction under control.

It was a good job she knew she wasn't good at being in a relationship—her previous boyfriends always found her lacking. She had promised to save herself the hurt of rejection and the disappointment of failing at something again by never having a romantic relationship again.

Not that a relationship was on offer from Rohan. Just because Rohan was standing next to her physically didn't mean he wasn't miles away from her. Developing a crush on Rohan was as pointless as fancying Michelangelo or his *David*.

It would be easier to deal with her unwanted crush if she wasn't in Rohan's company so much. But she couldn't exactly tell him to stay away. He was the crown prince; he didn't take orders from her.

CHAPTER FIVE

ROHAN SPENT THE morning attending government reporting sessions with his father. He then met his mother and sister for lunch. They hadn't been able to spend as much time together as he would have wanted. His mother was notionally overseeing the gala preparations which made her busier than usual.

She tried to get Rohan involved by insisting he have a say in the arrangements. Usually he tried to give his mother his full attention when she told him what had been organised because the gala was as important for him as it was to the rest of the family, but a large party was the furthest thing from his mind.

He was thinking about the regeneration project. And Priya. He thought about Priya a lot more than he should. According to her proposed scoping timetable, she would be visiting another mural today, the third. He missed having a chance to witness her reaction when she saw a mural for the first time. It was exactly the kind of reaction he hoped thousands of tourists would have one day.

'Is something wrong, Rohan,' his mother asked, clearly noticing his lack of concentration.

'I'm sorry, Ma. I was thinking about the summer palace. I hope there'll be time for me to take some of the guests round the sites.'

His mother didn't say anything. She pressed her lips together, but he wasn't sure whether it was because he'd annoyed her or whether she had something else on her mind.

'Do you know when you'll be able to present your proposal?' his sister asked.

'Not yet, there's still a lot of work to do before I get to that stage.' He frowned. His true desire was to convince his family to fund this regeneration project through investments and family finances, or at least the conservation work. At the moment, his father's opinion was if it went ahead, it would be a government-funded scheme. Which meant once Priya submitted her condition report, he would be assigned policy clerks who would then work with him to develop and cost the proposal fully. Only once that was complete would he be able to get an item on the annual agenda for further discussion. It could be years before the regeneration could start. Of course if his family financed the restoration work he wouldn't be able to use government clerks so he would have to work closely with Priya to develop the proposal.

It wouldn't be any hardship for him. She was intelligent, interesting and was as enthusiastic about the murals she'd seen so far as he was. He enjoyed the time he spent with her.

And she was easy on the eye.

He sat bolt upright. That was an inappropriate thought. She was here to perform a job. What she looked like was irrelevant and had no bearing on her ability to complete the work. How many times did he have to remind himself?

'Are you sure everything is okay, Rohan,' his mother asked again. 'You are acting quite strange.'

'Stranger than usual,' his sister added.

'I'm fine. Tell me about the Melwanis,' he said, naming a family of wealthy industrialists. He was interested in their work pioneering alternative fuel sources which could be valuable for Adysara's future sustainability. For his parents, the attraction was the Melwanis had two single daughters. Rohan knew what was expected from him at this gala and afterwards. His duty was to make a good marriage—getting his regeneration tourism proposal didn't alter the fact.

But since there was nothing he could do about his marriage prospects until the guests started arriving for the festivities, he could focus his attention on attracting investment into the island. And having cultural attractions for visitors would make the investment more likely.

After his meeting with his mother finished, Rohan returned to his rooms where he immediately asked a member of staff to bring him a light jacket and for his car to be brought round. He knew exactly which site Priya was supposed to be scoping.

Within half an hour, Rohan was standing behind Priya, watching as she was engrossed in conducting her condition survey. He stood as silently as he could, admiring how efficiently she carried out her examination.

She was so absorbed it was a good ten minutes before she noticed his presence. He liked how her instinctive reaction was to greet him as a good friend, before she remembered he was technically her client and royalty.

'How's it going?' he asked her, gesturing towards the mural.

'Good. This one probably won't take too long. I should be done in an hour.'

'Great. Will that be too much for you today or are you up to seeing the next one.'

She glanced at her watch, then put her hands on her hips. He was sure she hadn't intentionally drawn his attention to their shapely contour and the narrowness of her waist, but he had to force himself to drag his gaze away.

'If we can fit a small mural in today it would really help. I want to complete this part as soon as I can.'

'Bored of it already?' he teased her.

'Never,' she said with a grin which transformed her somewhat stern resting face to a vision of soft loveliness.

Suddenly he became aware she was looking at him. Was she waiting for a response? He'd missed what she said because he was admiring her features. He couldn't pretend he hadn't noticed she was beautiful. He'd worked with attractive people before and never let it distract him from the task at hand.

'I'm sorry, I shouldn't have expected you to know the exact size of the mural we'd go to next,' she said. 'The papers you gave me didn't have complete information so why should you know? And you're the prince so if you did have the data there's no reason for you to have it at instant recall.'

His lips quirked. He liked it when she began

wittering, almost talking to herself, each time she remembered he was royalty.

He reached out to put his hand on her arm, his intention was to reassure her his silence wasn't due to anything she said. But the moment he touched her skin, heat seared through him, like an electric jolt.

He took a step back. Her breath was shallow, she gave him a quick look of alarm then turned to her tools. Had she felt something too?

She was quiet, polite and reserved as she finished her work. But by the time they arrived at the next mural, she'd turned back to her natural self, excited to see what was in store.

He turned to look directly at her so he could take in her initial reaction. Instead of the open-mouthed awe he anticipated, she was looking...puzzled.

'Is everything all right, Priya?'

'Hmm.' She glanced at him briefly before returning her full attention on the mural so he repeated his question.

'Yes,' she replied, 'it's just this mural seems so familiar.'

Rohan looked at the wall painting. The central feature was a peacock displaying its train. In its glory days the colours would have been vibrant blues, greens and golds. But it was probably the simplest arrangement out of all of them.

'Peacocks are common in Indian art,' he offered.

She shook her head. 'It's the filigree plates on the corners, with the initials in them.' She pointed at them as she spoke. Slowly she began to smile. 'I think my didima told me about these. She must have visited them when she was a girl.'

'Your didima?' he asked, raising his eyebrows. She'd mentioned her grandmother on their first site visit. Perhaps the love of art had passed from grandmother to mother to daughter. 'Did she come to Adysara on holiday?'

Priya stared him, the wonder and delight of her realisation still shining from her expression. 'No, she was born on Adysara. Didn't I tell you that? I guess it makes me a quarter Adysarian. Fancy.'

He rarely met people who'd heard of Adysara; it seemed strangely fitting Priya would have a tie to his home country. Perhaps it explained why he felt so connected to her.

'Do you still have family on the island?' he asked.

'No, unfortunately. My didima's father emigrated to India for work and the family didn't come back.'

'You said you lost contact with your grandparents. That's a shame.'

'I know. But it's partly my fault because I didn't realise when their visits ended at first. My father remarried three years after mum passed away. I was hoping I could travel with my father and stepmother, the way I had while mum was alive. Or I was expecting to visit them during school holidays. That's why I thought my dadu and didima weren't visiting.' She grimaced. 'But I didn't see my father in the holidays and by the time I asked about my grandparents I couldn't contact them.'

'Your grandparents visits stopped around the same time as your father remarried?' he asked. At her nod, he furrowed his brow. It sounded like there was more going on behind the scenes than Priya knew. He made a note to ask his assistant to look into her didima— as an Adysarian. If her grandparents had no interest in meeting Priya then she wouldn't have to know. And it would be their loss.

'We've had a real problem with emigration over the years,' he said, as if they hadn't just had a personal conversation. 'Part of the reason I want this regeneration is to improve job prospects and make Adysara a great place to live and raise families, perhaps try to encourage immigration.'

'Oh, I think it would be wonderful,' she said before starting her examination of the mural.

As she worked, he heard her quietly humming a song from an animated film about lions.

He couldn't help chuckling. 'On the contrary, I'm in no rush to be king.'

Joy bubbled when, instead of being embarrassed she grinned back. 'Well of course not. Not when it means your father... Well you know.'

'My father's thinking of abdicating within five years. I could be king a lot sooner than I expected.' Now why had he told her when no one outside his family knew. He wasn't worried she would gossip about it to anyone in the palace. He trusted her implicitly.

Later that evening in his study he looked through some reports which had come through about the hotel companies he wanted as investors. Inevitably his thoughts turned to Priya again.

It was odd how he shared so much of his hopes and dreams with her. At first he thought it was because she was a stranger who understood his desire to show the world what his island had to offer while, at the same time, wanting to protect it and hide it so its glories would never diminish.

Was it his imagination or was there was another moment at the peacock mural when she'd asked him to pass her some equipment and their fingers had touched, their eyes locked, neither wanting to break the connection? The atmosphere was charged. Had she noticed? Could it be why she'd started avoiding looking at him directly when they talked? What would he do if she was attracted to him?

Nothing. She was technically an employee, despite not directly working for him. He had to ignore how stunning she was.

The problem was, this was something a little more than looks. He liked her. He enjoyed spending time in her company. She was beautiful. It wasn't surprising he was attracted to her. He had no intention of acting on it.

He wasn't in a position to offer her a relationship. All his previous relationships had inevitably been time limited. He made that clear to his girlfriends from the start, even though he hadn't always been completely honest it was his duty that prevented him from anything else.

But in this situation even a time-limited affair wasn't on the cards. In less than two months guests would be descending on his island, and among those guests was hopefully someone who would one day be his future wife. She might be a nameless, faceless person at the moment, but didn't he owe it to her, to himself, to his family, to only think about his guests. Increasing tourism and getting external investment didn't change anything for him in terms of the expectations people had of him.

Unless he made an advantageous marriage, Adysara's growth and prosperity would stagnate. Talented young people would continue to leave the island for better opportunities and slowly the population would decrease leading to further stagnation. He had a duty and he wasn't going to let anything get in the way of it. But to be on the safe side, he wouldn't go on any more visits with Priya.

CHAPTER SIX

IT HAD BEEN nine days since Priya had visited the final mural. Each one had been magnificent in its own right, but as a collection they were priceless. She could fully understand why Rohan believed Adysara could become a huge tourist destination with its glorious weather, golden beaches, crystal-clear warm waters. Its cultural heritage was the exquisite icing on top.

She was desperate to scope the caves. Rohan had said they would make the murals pale into insignificance—which she did find hard to believe. She was hoping to go later that day, depending on how far she got with her actual work. Sometimes it was difficult to concentrate on the palace murals when she knew what was outside, but she had to do her best, not only to hopefully demonstrate to Mac she was capable of working on the regeneration project—perhaps even leading it, but for the simple satisfaction of a job well done.

So far everything was progressing well, despite the disruptions being caused by the gala preparations, and her regular absences. Her team had already completed the restorations in the areas that were going to be used for the gala events and were now working on different areas, which, although still accessible by guests, weren't being used directly for any events. Mac was hoping they would be ready to begin the restoration to the artwork in the royal family's quarters. Since there weren't any murals in the royal wing she, personally, wouldn't be needed.

If the regeneration project didn't proceed, or she wasn't selected for it, there was a chance she would be returning to England in a matter of months.

She couldn't bear thinking about it. Because she would be missing out on a major work opportunity, there was no other reason.

She wondered whether Rohan…whether the prince would be accompanying her when they visited the caves. She'd enjoyed her time at the murals more when he was there, chatting with him and exchanging stories of their childhoods. He had seemed to be taking a personal interest in the work but hadn't accompanied her to the last few murals. She knew he was a busy man, but that hadn't stopped her disappointment.

As her mind started to relive her time with Rohan, Priya stretched and stood up. She took a step back to survey the work the team had accomplished that day.

She'd made some changes to the process they used, which took slightly longer but would make their effort more effective. So far it hadn't caused a substantial delay in their progress. Now, at least, when they left the palace, she could be reassured the preservation work would last more than the twenty years possible with the previous process.

She was packing away the tools and chemicals when a man, one of the palace workers came up to them.

'Madam,' he said, 'can you come with me, please?'

'Me?' Priya pointed to herself.

'Yes. Mr Agrawal has asked if he could speak to you if you've finished for the day?'

'Of course.' Priya turned to her colleagues. 'I guess I'll see you back at our quarters.'

'Would you like me to wait for you?' one of them asked with a worried expression.

She smiled. What did he think was going to happen to her? 'No, it's okay. I don't know how long I'm going to be and I'm sure you're eager to get back and wash and eat. Can you let Mac know I've been called to see Mr Agrawal, please?'

She followed the worker through long corridors, heading behind the large drawing rooms and lavish halls, now set up for the gala, careful to avoid disturbing anything. As they progressed, it was obvious how the decor was becoming less ostentatious as they moved towards the staff offices.

Still more extravagant than anything she'd experienced in her normal life, but there was definitely a difference.

She hoped the meeting with Mr Agrawal was to let her know when she would get a chance to see the caves. For a moment, her steps faltered. What if it wasn't the reason?

What if Mr Agrawal was unhappy with her changed process? She'd got Mac's approval but Leo Blake would have run everything by Mr Agrawal first. Regardless of the fact her team's project was going to have a more successful outcome because of her changes, she could have jeopardised any chance of remaining as team lead, and definitely any hope of taking on the role of project lead of the larger island work because she hadn't liaised with the palace's coordinator directly. It was such as foolish omission.

Or what if Mr Agrawal had become annoyed she was absent so often on the scoping visits. She'd been brought to Adysara specifically to take over from Leo Blake, not spend her time outside the palace. Or what if Rohan…the prince…complained about her informality and lack of professionalism?

She interlaced and unlaced her hands several times as she waited outside Mr Agrawal's room waiting for a response to her knock. The man who'd accompanied her nodded and left.

'Enter,' she heard.

The voice sounded familiar but it still startled her when she saw Rohan—no she had to start thinking of him as the crown prince again—standing by the desk. There was no one else in the room.

'Yuvaraja-sahib, I was expecting to see Mr Agrawal.'

He looked stern. 'Didn't I tell you to call me Rohan?'

She grimaced. 'I don't feel right calling you by your first name in the palace, Yuvaraja.' He pressed his lips together. 'In case someone hears me or I forget and use your first name in front of others and they think I'm being over-familiar. I'm quite new as team lead, I don't want to single myself out.'

'Fine. But don't call me yuvaraja or sahib, please. If you don't want to call me Rohan you can call me Mr Varma. I would ask anyone in your team to call me the same if we spoke directly.'

Priya gave a brief nod of acknowledgement, pleased he accepted her feelings above his own request—it wasn't something she was used to.

'How has your work on the murals gone?' he asked.

'Good.' She gave him a brief rundown of her initial findings and thoughts. 'I should be able to let you have my report within a couple of weeks.'

'That's quick,' he remarked.

Priya bit her lip and smiled self-consciously. 'It's such a thrilling project, I'm too enthusiastic to waste any time. I've been working on my report every evening.'

He grinned at her. Her heart seemed to skip a beat at the warmth of his smile. Her reaction was wholly inappropriate for the situation and she had to ignore how attractive the man was. He was her client. Not to mention a prince.

'I felt the same way when I first saw the

caves. Come round here, please,' he said, indicating his side of the table where schematics were laid out in front of him. 'This shows where the caves are on Adysarina Island. There's one main stretch of four caves around this range. Then a few other areas around the other islands. Eight in total I think are worth scoping. My favourite sculpture is in this cave.' He indicated with his finger. 'Cave six. It's a little bit off the beaten path so if we did open it to the public we would have to create a new roadway. I think it will be worth it. We could start with it, but I think I'll build up your anticipation before I take you there.'

'Oh, will you be coming with me?'

Her heart started to race again at the thought of getting to talk with him, hear his ideas and stories about the island, laugh with him, be close to him. She sighed. She was doing it again.

It's a crush. You don't do relationships and definitely not with royalty. Be sensible. Don't spoil the chance to work on this project because there happens to be an attractive man in the vicinity. Behave!

'I asked Agrawal to pull out all the historical documents we have about the caves,' he said, indicating some papers. 'Will you be able to go out tomorrow, or do you need some time to organise things with your team?'

Priya mentally ran through the work she had scheduled for the following day. With a small amount of rejigging she should be able to be away without having too great an impact on the work.

She explained that to him, adding, 'But I do need to confirm with Mac.' She didn't want to risk any possibility Mac would think she was shirking her job as team leader. Mac had told her, when she first discussed the prince's project with him, he was happy for her to spend time scoping out the work—particularly if it meant their company would be considered for the job. But she always remembered she wasn't first choice as the team leader, and when Leo Blake's emergency was over she could be sent back to England just as easily as she was brought over.

'Of course.' His eyebrows lifted and a brief smile played on his mouth.

Priya blushed. It probably was a safe assumption her boss wouldn't refuse a request from the prince, but she wasn't going to take anything for granted. It was too important.

'How should I let you know?' she asked. 'Shall I send a message via one of the workers?'

He furrowed his brow. 'Come with me, back to my study.'

Curious she followed him out of the room. She quickly realised there had to be back corridors for the staff since the path he took to his study was much more direct than the way she'd been brought that first evening, and more richly decorated. Another stark reminder, if she needed it, despite the things they had in common, their lives were light years apart.

Once in Rohan's quarters, he asked her to remain in his waiting room while he went into his study. Priya took the time to look around the room, something she'd been too nervous to do the last time she was there.

The modern, bright furniture should have looked incongruous against the old architecture but it blended together seamlessly. Rohan's study was designed in a similar style but his desk was old, reminding her of the Resolute desk.

'Sorry about that,' Rohan said, popping his head through the interconnecting door. 'Come through. It will be a few minutes. Take a seat.' He indicated the comfortable sofa arrangement at the side of his study, rather than the seat opposite his desk. 'I'm sorry, I realised I must have kept you from your evening meal. I've asked for some food to be brought.'

Priya was overwhelmed by his thoughtfulness. 'You didn't have to do that. There's always food around and they keep a fully stocked fridge for us so I could make myself something if I need to.'

'There's always plenty of food around,' he said, waving his hand in a gesture of dismissal. 'I've also asked for someone to bring you a new mobile phone, specifically to contact me directly. You're going to have to complete some paperwork about non-disclosures and confidentially on threat of death which you'll have to sign with a blood print.'

His expression and tone were so sincere, Priya couldn't do anything but stare at him until he finally broke into a huge grin, laughing at her alarm. She joined in, giggling at her own gullibility.

'Anyway,' Rohan said, leaning back in his armchair, 'tell me what you thought of the last few murals. Not their condition. I can wait for the report. Tell me how they made you feel.'

She hoped her conversation made sense because all she could focus on was the idea she would have direct access to Rohan, she could phone him or send him messages. It was a special link between them.

And she was being ridiculous again, letting her attraction rule her common sense. She had to maintain distance and professionalism at all costs.

'You don't need to accompany me to the caves,' she said, hesitantly. 'I know you must have a lot to do. I'm sure the papers you've given me will be enough.'

She held her breath, dreading his response, but not entirely sure which option she dreaded.

CHAPTER SEVEN

ROHAN HAD BEEN stuck indoors for days finalising the sale of his business and divesting himself of all investments which could impact his role as maharajah in the future. Sooner than he planned, if his father kept to his stated intention of retiring, or abdicating, in five years.

Not to mention, with the gala a little over a month away, his involvement in the preparations was increasing with more frequent fittings for his suits, going over the arrangements for the events with his mother and with the different coordinators for the various activities. On top of which he continued to have regular discussions with his family about the lineage and advantages of the female guests.

He knew his duty, and he would perform it willingly and happily, but sometimes he just wished the gala could happen without all this disruption in the run-up to the event.

And if that wasn't enough to interrupt his plans, the art restorers were getting ready to work on his family's quarters. One of his favourite paintings had been removed from the wall and taken down to the studios. It was a shame the royal rooms didn't have any murals. He wouldn't accidentally bump into Priya.

He wondered how her scoping visits were going. He hadn't accompanied her since they went to the first cave. A clear image came to mind of her face when she first saw the stone cuttings. Entranced—her full lips forming a perfect O.

He'd been training his lamp on her instead of the wall and when she'd reached out to direct his hand to the spots she wanted to illuminate, his skin had felt hot under her fingers, his mouth going dry and his lungs forgetting how to breathe.

All from a simple touch, which she'd done without thinking; she'd dropped her hand quickly enough when she'd realised.

He sensed she was keeping her distance from him. She'd been politely professional on the visit, something he wouldn't usually mind, but he'd missed her openness, her unguarded chattiness when they were together before.

Since then he'd been so caught up in palace affairs he'd had no choice but to stay away. But it had been a week. He could do with a day away from the busyness of the palace and going to the caves always helped his mood. Priya being at the caves was simply a chance to kill two birds with one stone.

But since they would be together, it would be pleasant to share a meal again. If they took a picnic they could stay at the site longer. Rohan called his staff to make the necessary arrangements.

The following day, Rohan paced around the mouth of the cave. At first he'd been inside with Priya while she was examining the stone-cut architecture, but she explained his presence could affect the humidity and she needed a baseline reading. He left her to it, trusting her when she said it helped with the preservation.

It was a shame, because he'd enjoyed observing her as she worked, fully focussed on the task at hand. He suspected she wouldn't notice if a herd of elephants trampled across the cave, his presence was completely ignored.

He waited for her impatiently until she finally surfaced, a bright smile on her face.

'I know I sound like a broken record, but

what you have on this island is beyond anything I've seen before. It's a privilege to be able to work on this,' she said.

Without waiting for his response, she went to sit on a rock and began to write some notations.

He went to the car to collect the picnic lunch and water cooler. He'd sent the driver and his bodyguard to wait in the shade, lower down the road, but they both started to move towards him when he reached the car so he put his hand up to stop them.

He could imagine Priya's reaction if he couldn't carry his own lunch and water. And part of him didn't want the others around while they ate. He wanted to chat with Priya and try to close the distance between them.

She was still writing when he came back, her tongue poking out the corner of her mouth. He wished it was his tongue tracing the contours of her full, shapely lips. Alarmed at the direction of his thoughts, he put down the picnic basket and hurried inside the cave.

There he took a few deep breaths as he tried to concentrate on the stone carving of a tiger in front of him but all he could think about was the image of Priya, sitting on a rock like a modern-day goddess.

Was that why he was spending this time

with her? Because he was attracted to her, desired her? She was a beautiful woman. He'd noticed how stunning the first time he saw her but on an objective level, as he'd appreciate a fine painting. He hadn't thought there was anything more to it.

She was right when she'd told him he didn't need to come with her. He tried telling himself he was concerned about the project, it was too important not to deal with it personally, but it wasn't true. Certainly not to the extent he was letting other things build up on his desk and leaving the palace when gala arrangements were moving at an accelerated pace.

If she was similarly attracted to him was irrelevant—he couldn't do anything about it. His priority should be concentrating on the hundreds of single women who would soon be arriving on Adysara—any one of which would make a suitable wife and queen. The last thing he should be doing right now was going out of his way to spend time with Priya Sen. After this visit he would turn the project over to someone else or ask for government permission to let Mr Agrawal lead on it.

Rohan paused, his eyes roving over the carvings. He really wanted to show Priya his favourite cave. Number six. He wanted to watch her expressions as she took in the stone cuttings in the cave for the first time. He wanted to hear her initial, unfiltered reaction. And when he took her through to see what he considered would be the showpiece of the whole island...

'Rohan,' Priya's voice called from the cave entrance. 'Are you okay down there? Aren't you coming to eat?'

'Yes, I'll be right out,' he called back. Whatever he was feeling, he couldn't let Priya suspect he wanted her. Unless she already did, and that was the reason she was distancing herself.

He joined her by the rock where she was helping his bodyguard lay out plates and cutlery on a small trestle table. There were also two folding chairs open next to the table. Once they were done, his bodyguard left them.

As Rohan sat down, he caught Priya's amused glance.

'What is it?' he asked.

'Oh, I don't think I should say,' she replied, shaking her head with exaggerated fake apprehension.

'Well, now you have to say.'

'When you mentioned you'd organise a picnic lunch for today I was imagining sandwiches on a rug. Not this.' She gesticulated at the table and glass containers with meat and vegetable curries, luchis, naans and salads. Even though she was mumbling under her breath as she opened one of the containers, he heard her say, 'I guess the royal bottom can't sit on the ground.'

He let out a deep chuckle. 'I'll have you know this royal bottom can endure some discomfort.'

Her eyes widened and colour flooded her cheeks as she realised he'd heard her, but she gave him a shy, embarrassed smile. She was enchanting.

'Of course, we have to take extra precautions here,' he continued, 'because the insurance won't pay out if the royal bottom is injured through careless action.'

He struggled to maintain his serious expression when her mouth fell open. 'You've insured your...' she said, waving her hand in his direction.

He threw his head back and gave a hearty laugh. 'You're so easy to tease.'

She closed her eyes and shook her head slowly, but her smiled proved she wasn't upset. 'You know you're lucky there aren't bread rolls here or I'd have lobbed one at you.'

He shrugged. 'That would be treason.'

'It would be worth it.' She finished opening the last container. 'Is the royal personage capable of serving himself or would you like me to wait on you?'

He titled his head pretending to consider her question. 'Hmm, I'll be able to manage. In fact, to prove it I'll serve you.' Before she could protest, he stood and began holding out dishes for her inspection, enjoying playing the role of butler, hamming it up as if he was performing in a British historical drama.

They chatted as they ate, their conversation flowing easily.

It had been a long time since he felt so relaxed with someone, as if he'd known them for a lifetime instead of days.

She was intelligent, interesting, curious, passionate, beautiful. He liked her. But it wasn't as simple as it sounded.

During their conversation they often referred to his royal status—he didn't usually bring it up outside the family. He never liked to distinguish himself from the people he was with. But with Priya, it was almost a form of protection. A reminder because of who he was he had a duty to marry someone who could help the island improve and grow, he wasn't free to choose who he liked.

If it had been any other time he might have asked Priya out for a meal. Perhaps they would have dated for a while. But inevitably it would end, because all his relationships had to. This time there was no point entertaining the thought of a brief relationship. In a few short weeks, guests would be arriving at the palace for a gala event and he would be expected to charm potential brides.

If he hadn't been Rohan Varma, Yuvaraja of Adysara, duty-bound to marry someone who could improve the prosperity of the island and improve the quality of life of its people, but just plain Rohan Varma, maybe things could have been different. He suspected the end would always be the same though. He didn't see any reason to get married apart from carrying out his duty. He wasn't going to fall in love. It was something he didn't believe was real or lasting. Sooner or later, just being together wouldn't be enough and the woman could start to want something he couldn't give.

It was a moot point. He wasn't plain Rohan Varma. His romantic future wasn't in his control.

CHAPTER EIGHT

SITTING NEXT TO Rohan in the back of the Jeep, she could feel the anticipation and excitement emanating from him. Cave six was the one he was most excited about, the one he considered to be particularly special. Since all the caves she'd already inspected had been sensational, she couldn't wait to see how magnificent this one would be.

She glanced at Rohan and caught him looking directly at her. She gave him a shy smile, but his face was severe. What had changed from only seconds before?

After today, she didn't know when or if she would see him again. A huge, painful knot twisted inside her at the thought.

She would miss spending time with him. If he wasn't Rohan Varma, Crown Prince of Adysara, she may have tried to keep in touch, found a way of holding on to the phone he'd given her. She wanted to get to know him better still.

No. She shook the possibility from her mind. It didn't matter who he was. She wasn't looking for a relationship. She was wary of them.

She was only interested in doing her job. Exceeding expectations so she was even in the running for better career opportunities. It's what she needed to concentrate on now.

Her attraction to Rohan was an inconvenience she had to ignore.

But sometimes, with the way Rohan looked at her and the way he spoke to her, she couldn't help sensing he felt something for her too. Although it was probably wishful thinking.

Experience, in the form of her last couple of boyfriends, taught her she was difficult to love. Her own father didn't care enough about her.

A member of royalty wasn't going to suddenly develop feelings for her.

'Are we almost there?' she asked, like a child who'd got bored of a journey.

'Hmm?' Rohan was obviously miles away from her in his thoughts. 'Sorry. I missed what you asked?'

'I was wondering whether we were close by.' She gestured outside the window. 'I noticed the topography has changed. We're moving into a more elevated terrain.'

Rohan looked out the window. 'Yes, we're

almost here.' He sat forward in his seat—the excitement and anticipation was back.

The car stopped. Once again, Rohan gave the driver and bodyguard permission to wander round so they didn't have to stay with the car.

They were at a hillside with a number of man-formed entrances carved into the side.

Rohan reached for her hand. He led her down a narrow gap that didn't appear to be a cave mouth at first but widened as they went further.

'The main cave is through here,' he explained. 'There are a number of interconnected chambers and passageways. Access might be a problem but believe me it will be worth it. We'll probably need to have restricted guided tours down here.'

While Rohan spoke about the issues concerning opening the caves to the public, Priya was only conscious of the warmth emanating from her hand, sending sparks along her arms. The sensual thrill should have alarmed her and made her remove her hand, but it felt so safe, and secure; perfectly enveloped by his.

The stone cuttings she'd examined so far were in excellent condition considering their environment. But the darkness had probably helped delay any deterioration. Once light and heat, caused by a number of visitors, impacted the cave then decay could be rapid if they didn't get the preservation process right.

'Close your eyes,' Rohan said, turning to her just before they reached the end of the tunnel.

'What?' Priya asked. 'It's dark enough, isn't it?'

'Please.' He looked like a child trying to cajole more chocolate from his parent.

She giggled. 'Fine.' She made an exaggerated showing of closing her eyes, jutting her face out for his inspection. A warm hand covered her eyes. 'Rohan. Is it necessary? Don't you trust me?'

'Always.'

His succinct response touched her. She felt him move so he was behind her, one hand still over her eyes. He put his other hand on her shoulder and gently guided her forward.

Her skinned burned where his fingers made contact, his body so close she could feel his breath whisper against her with every exhale. Her steps faltered as she tried to control the explosive currents coursing through her.

'Almost there,' Rohan said after they'd taken a few paces. He carefully moved her and turned her to her right. 'Keep your eyes closed,' he instructed as he removed his hand from over her eyes and stepped away.

Priya felt air begin to circulate around her. She wasn't sure whether it was because the space around her was larger or because she was no longer in such close proximity to Rohan. She instinctively moved as if searching for him.

'Wait,' he admonished. 'Be still. You're in the perfect spot. Ready?'

She nodded.

'Okay. Open your eyes now,' he said.

Slowly, Priya raised her lids. She was staring at an intricately carved tableau of multiple figures of different shapes and sizes forming a circle around a centrepiece. The carved figures were in rows, with one row standing on the shoulders of the figures below. Each was carrying something—a musical instrument, parchment, baskets containing grass, probably rice, stones, or classical weapons. The centrepiece consisted of a larger bovine creature, not a cow or a buffalo, maybe a mithun. The animal was carrying a small child whose hands were raised up, holding a globe-shaped structure splitting to reveal a tiny plant shoot. The whole piece depicted the variety of people which made up Adysara; which made up a country. It was a celebration of life and death and rebirth.

There were small, discrete carvings around the rest of the cave which complemented the tableau of the main wall.

It would be a crime to risk letting this craftsmanship be damaged by the footfall of tourists. But it would also be a crime to keep this hidden from the world. Photos would never do it justice.

Her hands itched to trace the detailed contours along the carvings, but her professional instincts overrode inclination, knowing the barest trace of oil from her fingers could degrade the work.

She turned her head to see Rohan, who was watching her expectantly.

'I can see why this is your favourite,' she whispered, reverently.

He shook his head, surprising her. 'That's not all of it. Come on, I want to show you. You need to close your eyes again but we're going through another passageway first.'

Priya's anticipation mounted. If the crowning glory of the cave wasn't the tableau in front of her, she couldn't imagine what lay in store.

Again she followed Rohan through a dark man-constructed corridor until he told her to stop and close her eyes, at which point he guided her forwards.

'Almost there,' he said.

She sensed, from the change of air, they had come through to an open area. And she was certain she could feel the sun on her. Had they walked out of the cave? Was what he wanted to show her outside?

This time, after he had positioned her where he wanted, he came to stand next to her.

'Open your eyes,' he whispered in her ear.

The sensations rushing through her body at the heated breath from his voice rendered her momentarily incapable of movement.

She quickly opened her eyes to dispel those feelings. Trying to get her bearings, she almost couldn't take in what was in front of her.

'Priya?' Rohan said in an uncertain tone.

She forced herself to focus on the shape in front of her.

'Oh, my!' she said, as soon as her mind was able to process she was actually standing next to a megalith, carved from the cliff face, of a palace guarded by tigers and lions at each of its corners. She instinctively reached for Rohan's hand, as if he could somehow ground her.

She'd had no idea this existed. It was much smaller than the Kailasha temple in the Ellora caves, of course, but it could rival its artistry.

It felt completely natural to walk around the megalith with her hand in Rohan's. Occasionally, whenever she squealed because her eye landed on a particularly intricate or unexpected carving, Rohan would squeeze her hand, grinning at her obvious enthusiasm.

It was almost as if they were just a couple of ordinary tourists, viewing one of the most impressive stone-cut megaliths in the world and she wasn't Priya Sen, conservator, walking with her kind of client who also happened to be the crown prince of the island.

With that reminder, she almost flung his hand away. He blinked, but she didn't miss the brief flash of hurt in his eyes. She stepped towards the structure and pretended to examine the ground for signs of deterioration.

Why did it have to be Rohan who caused these feelings in her? She'd already decided to focus on her career. She wanted to be project lead on this work. She was trying to prove she was capable.

She wasn't looking for romance. And if she was, Rohan would be the last person who would be suitable. Even if he was interested in her, and she couldn't believe it was a remote possibility, he was so far out of her orbit. He could never be hers.

Everybody knew he was searching for his

future wife—the next Maharani of Adysara. He wasn't going to give it up to have a quick affair with Priya.

And she couldn't let her attraction to him distract her from her goal. Her work was everything to her. It had to be.

Forcing herself to concentrate on carrying out her investigations she took out some equipment and worked diligently for a while. She came across a section which she could use Rohan's assistance for, so she turned around to ask him to help.

He had moved back to stand in the shadow of the surrounding rocks. The powerful set of his shoulders and his broad chest cast a long shadow over the rocks which, though imposing, made her feel protected and safe.

She wished she had the artistic skills to commit this gorgeous specimen of a man to posterity.

Something above him caught her attention.

Without thinking, she leapt in his direction, throwing her arms around him and pushing them both out of the way. She heard a small thud behind her from where the object she'd glimpsed falling towards Rohan had landed. She slowly became aware she had her arms around him and he had, at some point, thrown his arms around her.

She was in Rohan's arms. And she felt like she belonged there. She never wanted to leave.

She was in Rohan's arms because he had been in danger—the implication of that renewed her alarm.

She pushed herself out of his arms and began pacing.

'This is dangerous. You shouldn't be here. If something happened to you…' Her voice trailed off as her imagination played out the frightening possibilities.

'Nothing happened. I'm all right.' He reached for her but she kept out of his grasp.

'All right? What if I hadn't reached you in time. We shouldn't have come. *You* shouldn't have come.'

Rohan walked over to the stone on the ground. 'Come over here. Look at it.'

Priya walked to stand next to him. In the scheme of things, the stone was small and wouldn't have done any major harm if it had hit Rohan, but that could be luck. There could be larger rocks on the brink of tumbling towards them.

'You should get out of here,' she said, pushing him in the direction of the exit. 'There's no need for you to join me. I can work on my own. It's too big a risk.'

'It was a small, displaced stone. The cave walls aren't coming down.'

Priya shook her head. 'This could have been so bad.'

'But it wasn't.'

'If something had happened it would have been my fault.'

'It would have been an accident.'

'I would have been blamed. What if they didn't believe it was an accident? What if they thought I was trying to assassinate you?'

Rohan made a choking sound.

'Could I be tried for treason?'

'Priya, nothing happened.'

'You shouldn't be here. You need to leave.'

'It's okay. Calm down.' He pulled her back into his arms until they were standing so close together no light could be seen between them.

She inhaled deeply a couple of times, her heart rate gradually returning to normal.

Home.

The word resounded in her mind. Followed closely by alarm bells.

Her rational mind told her she had to move. She had to get away from him. This wasn't her place and Rohan wasn't her home.

But he could have been injured. Concern tore through her heart. And it wasn't because he was a client. And it wasn't even because he was the crown prince.

It was because she cared about him.

She began to tremble. As he stroked her back to calm her, the sensations flooding through her body soon switched from concern to desire.

'Are you okay?' he asked in a low voice.

'I think so.' She took a deep breath but a picture of Rohan lying on the ground knocked out by a rock filled her imagination. She tightened her arms around him.

She felt the lightest touch against her hair. She slowly lifted her head. He was gazing tenderly at her.

Her lips parted as his head descended, inviting his kiss.

The spark between them ignited as their mouths met. They leaned into each other, their bodies pressed tight.

Soon, their kisses became greedy as if they were taking life-sustaining oxygen from each other.

It was powerful, dynamic, sensual, imbued with feelings.

And it shouldn't have happened.

Later that evening in his study, Rohan relived their kiss. He didn't know what would have happened if his bodyguard hadn't called out to them from inside the cave, asking if they were ready for lunch.

He hadn't expected the conflagration that flared between them, but Rohan hoped he would have had the decency to stop the kiss before it went too far—he wouldn't have actually given in to the temptation to lay her on the ground and make love to her in front of his favourite rock sculpture. And now he would never know.

Because it could never happen again.

He had nothing to offer her. He wasn't free to enter into a relationship with her. In a few weeks he would be meeting lots of woman, any one of whom could be his future wife. He couldn't suggest a brief fling—that would be unconscionable behaviour.

After his bodyguard's interruption, they'd returned to the car. Priya had claimed she was feeling faint from heat and asked to return to the palace. During the journey home, she refused to meet his gaze.

He hadn't attempted to engage her in conversation then, but he needed to make sure she was all right so he'd asked a member of staff to request she join him after dinner and was now pacing his study waiting for her.

It felt like hours before he heard a knock at

the door. He rushed to it, pulling it open with unnecessary force.

Priya took a startled step back. He drank in her beauty, hoping to read her thoughts in her deep eyes, but she still refused to meet his gaze.

'Come in,' he said, as he nodded his dismissal to her escort.

She went to stand in front of his desk, her head bowed as if she'd been summoned before the headmaster.

He went to his seating area and called her over. He knew how important her job was to her and he had to reassure her that her rejection of their kiss would have no impact on her work for the palace.

'Priya,' he began once they were both seated.

'I'm so sorry, Rohan,' she said, giving him a quick glance before looking down at the hands she was wringing. 'I should never have done it. Please excuse me. Chalk it up to the circumstances. It was relief when I thought you could be injured.'

Rohan crossed his legs as he leaned back against the couch. 'You're apologising to me?'

'Yes. I'm sorry.'

'About kissing me?'

'Of course. It was completely inappropriate of me to have done that, I should—'

'But I kissed you.'

She did look at him then. 'No, you didn't. I started it.'

'I did,' he replied.

'No! It was me,' she argued back.

He grinned. Only with Priya would he be arguing about who was responsible for initiating the most incredible kiss he'd ever experienced. His smile faltered. Their kiss may have been incredible, but he had to make sure she knew it could never happen again.

'Priya, let's just agree it was mutual,' he said, putting up his hand when it looked like she was going to continue arguing. She gave him a tight nod. 'But it was wrong. It shouldn't have happened. I'm sorry.'

She bent her head, not saying anything.

'I'm sorry,' he repeated. He didn't know what else to say. He couldn't tell her he was attracted to her. Couldn't let her know he liked her, he admired her, he loved spending time with her. It was all true but he couldn't act on it. He needed to stay away from her. Otherwise he could be accused of leading her on.

Her stomach growled. He chuckled at her embarrassed expression. She covered her midsection with her hands as if doing so would stop the noise, but all it did was draw his attention to the apex of her thighs.

He blinked to clear the direction of his thought. 'Haven't you had dinner?' he asked. 'I didn't expect you to miss it to come here.'

'I didn't. I wasn't hungry. I haven't had much of an appetite since...' She trailed off.

He didn't have to be a mind-reader to understand what she meant.

'Come on,' he said, getting to his feet. Instinctively he put his hand out to help her but pulled it back. Reducing physical contact between them was essential.

Rohan led Priya out of the study into his private living quarters and down the corridor to the kitchenette. He rarely used it, but it was always kept fully stocked with ingredients to make a simple meal.

Priya glanced around. 'What are we doing in here?'

'Getting you something to eat.'

'Oh, that's okay. I can get something when I get back to my rooms.'

'No, I insist.'

She looked uncomfortable.

'What's the problem?' he asked.

'I don't want to bother any of your staff. I'd rather make something when I get back.'

'I'm not going to call someone.'

She released a breath of relief. 'Of course, if you don't mind me cooking something here, I'll see what there is. Have you eaten or shall I make something for you too?' she asked, walking towards the fridge.

'Sit,' Rohan said, pointing to the small table in the corner of the room. 'I'll make you something?'

'You can't do that!'

'I can cook. I did live independently when I was abroad you know. And I didn't resort to takeout every evening.'

'I'm sure you're very capable,' Priya replied, with a slight roll of her eyes. 'But I can't let you cook for me. It's not right.'

He didn't know why it was so important to him Priya didn't think he was someone who spent his days being waited on hand and foot. Rationally, it would make more sense if he did emphasise the difference in their status.

But he valued her good opinion of him.

'Let's compromise,' he suggested. 'We can make something together. Eggs is probably the fastest. What about with sausages or some omelette.'

'Omelette.'

He pulled out some eggs, onions and chillies and spices while Priya looked for the pan and cooking utensils.

'Is this okay or would you prefer something different in your omelette?' he checked.

Priya looked at his ingredients. His forehead furrowed when he saw her lips tremble.

'Priya?' he asked, with concern.

She gave him a tremulous smile. 'My mum used to make omelettes like this. I haven't had them for years. Thank you. It brings her back to me.'

He puffed his chest out, as if he'd accomplished something monumental, rather than being lucky in his choice of fillings.

'I'll chop, you whisk,' Priya said. When he would have reached for the knife she swatted his hand away. 'I'm not going to risk you getting a knife injury now. Not after this morning.'

He swallowed, his mind instantly reliving their kiss. From the faint blush in her cheeks, he hoped she was also remembering. He turned away. Cooking together in such intimate circumstances wasn't the wisest decision when part of the reason he'd asked her to come to his study was to reinforce why any relationship between them was impossible.

Rohan sighed. He still hadn't broached the subject fully. He looked over at Priya standing at the hob, turning their omelettes. Foolish though he knew it was, he didn't want to ruin the small scene of domesticity. But he had to.

'Priya,' he said. 'We need to talk.'

Priya straightened her shoulders. What could this be about? She'd already apologised for kissing him. What more could she do? Should she apologise again?

She still had trouble believing they'd kissed. She'd claimed her action was a result of thinking he was in danger. That heightens the emotions. Makes people react out of character. That's all it was. But the truth was, she'd been dreaming of kissing him, oh, for days now.

But what happened was so different from her dreams. She could still feel the pressure of his lips on hers, the warmth of his breath. The strength of his arms around her.

She closed her eyes savouring the moment again. When she lifted her lids, she met his penetrating gaze. It took her an immense effort to tear her eyes away. They needed to talk, he'd said. And he was right.

'What did you want to say?' she asked.

'About what happened today…'

'I've already said sorry. I promise it won't happen again.'

'I don't know if that's true.'

She jerked back. That was a concern. As

much as she was attracted to Rohan, she knew there was no prospect of a relationship. Now there was a risk her behaviour had affected his inclination to work with her. Although the scoping work could be completed on her own, if she got the chance to lead the project, which was still a big *if* she knew, then she would probably have to report to Rohan on a regular basis.

'I know it was unprofessional,' she began.

'That's not what I mean.'

'Then?'

'In my opinion it's always best to be open and honest in these situations. Prevarication doesn't help anything.'

'Okay.'

'We kissed. We both know it can never happen again.'

Priya nodded. Hadn't they already agreed this?

'I like you. I think you're beautiful. In any other situation I would be interested in exploring a short relationship.'

Priya's jaw dropped. She wasn't expecting that. His wide eyes told her the words came as a surprise to him too.

'But I'm not in a position to do anything.'

Not in a position? What a strange way to

phrase things. It sounded like it was outside
his control.

'I can't start anything with you because it
wouldn't be fair, to you, or to my future wife.
You've probably heard rumours this year's
gala is a particularly special event for me as
Yuvaraja of Adysara because I'm expected
to get married soon and hopefully someone
suitable will be at the gala.'

She nodded.

'It wouldn't be fair to start anything with
you because the most I could offer was a fling
for a couple of weeks.'

What he was saying was reasonable. She
understood his position, but she couldn't help
being curious. 'Is that what you want or are
you just doing your duty?'

Rohan pursed his lips. 'Doing my duty is
what I want. I'm not being forced to marry
anyone in particular. I get a choice. And I
hope true affection with my wife will come
with time.'

'Affection, not love?' she asked, before bit-
ing her lip. Why was she bringing up love?

'I don't believe romantic love exists. It's a
hormonal myth. A lie people say to excuse
some of their behaviour. I do believe a com-
paniable love can arise after time together,

which is just as easily done after marriage as before.'

Again he sounded completely reasonable. And she had certainly been fooled when she thought she'd loved her previous boyfriends. She thought she'd never get over them at the time but in reality, those feelings passed fairly quickly.

'So you understand, Priya. There are expectations and responsibility that come with my position. I have a duty to make a suitable marriage. I cannot start anything with you.'

She bent her head. She didn't need to be a genius to work out he was telling her she wasn't suitable for a prince. She just wanted to curl up into a ball and hide. She didn't need another reminder she wasn't good enough.

CHAPTER NINE

PRIYA TOOK A step out of the final cave. That was it. She was finished with the scoping exercise. Now all she had to do was write up the report and submit it to Rohan.

Her heart felt heavy at the thought of Rohan. He hadn't accompanied her for any more visits. She hadn't expected it, not after their conversation, when he'd categorically told her she wasn't good enough to be in a relationship with him. If she hadn't kissed him, if she hadn't made it so obvious how attractive she found him, perhaps he would still be coming to the sites with her. She packed up her belongings and got into the car.

She couldn't regret their kiss. It felt like it was the first time, like she'd never been kissed before. Automatically, her hand went to her mouth trying to recapture the memory of his lips. No, she couldn't regret it. Even if her wholly inappropriate reaction meant she was on her own.

She sighed. It didn't matter. She was used to being alone. The stone sculptures were all the company she needed. Her work was all she wanted.

Her dream job had come true when she was asked to take over from Leo as team leader on the palace preservation work. But now she had a new aspiration, which was to work on the preservation of these stone cuttings. It was exactly what attracted her to conservation work in the first place. If she could lead on the work...it would be the pinnacle of her career.

She needed to pull herself together. She had to quash all thoughts of Rohan and get over these feelings she didn't completely understand. Instead she needed to focus her attention on showing she was capable. She hoped Mac and Mr Agrawal would notice. She wasn't ready yet to put herself out there and risk rejection by broaching the idea of staying on herself.

Rohan had to stay out of the picture. It was rare for her to meet someone she felt in sync with and how totally natural and completely herself she was in his company. It wasn't that she sometimes forgot about the difference in their status—it was she sometimes forgot she hadn't known him for years.

She expelled a deep, lonely breath. If only he had been anyone but the crown prince of Adysara—someone who actually lived in her world.

But it was probably better this way. Any relationship would have inevitably fizzled out. They always did. It didn't matter who the guy was. She just didn't have what it took to sustain a relationship.

She had decided long ago, after her last boyfriend broke up with her, she wasn't the kind of person who would have a husband and children; she wasn't the kind of person who deserved to be loved.

She was determined her career would be her whole focus. And she loved what she did with a passion she hadn't expected. She loved the impact what she did had on the world's heritage.

One day, if she kept trying she would be the lead on one of these conservation projects. Perhaps it wouldn't be the one on the island; despite every effort she would make, she wasn't sure she would be picked over someone like Leo. But one day, with hard work and determination, she might be considered for another major lead position. That was her future. She couldn't let anything derail that. It was all she had.

Back at her quarters, she received a message asking her to go to Mr Agrawal's office. Her heart leapt. Was it really a request from Rohan? Did he want to speak to her? Had he missed her as much as she missed him?

She was slightly surprised to see Mac waiting for her outside their quarters. Disappointment flooded over her when she found out he was also going to see Mr Agrawal. As they walked over, she quickly gave him an update on the scoping work, expecting it was the reason she was invited to the meeting.

Before they got to Mr Agrawal's office, Mac halted her.

'You've been here over a month now, haven't you?' he asked.

'That's right.'

'Are you enjoying it?'

'Very much,' she replied, her expression brightening up thinking about the work. Was this the right moment to bring up her desire to continue as team leader? She took a deep breath, then let it out and shrank back a little. No, she shouldn't put herself forward in such a way.

'With the work in the palace and the site visits you've worked through the weekends and haven't taken any time off. You must need some time to relax.'

'Oh, I haven't felt that way,' she hastened to reassure him. 'We've got the public holidays with the gala coming up. And with the site visits, I've been touring round the island so it's like time off.'

'But it isn't, Priya. You should take this weekend off. In fact take Friday and Monday too—have a long weekend. Tomorrow, after you've finished for the day give me a status update and then you can start your leave. Rest and relax, ready to get back refreshed on Tuesday.'

'It's not necessary. The team have had to deal with my absence when I was on the site visits already. I shouldn't take more time away.'

'I insist. Priya, I'm responsible for your well-being while we're here. You wouldn't let any of your team work continuously without taking any time off would you?'

'Certainly not,' she replied. Although the work in the palace didn't stop over the weekends, she always checked the roster to make sure people were taking time off.

His look was enough to show there was no arguing with him. Like it or not she was going to have an enforced long break.

She didn't know what she was going to do with the free time. Perhaps visit the megalith again if she was allowed. At the very least, she could get most of the report written up.

During their meeting with Mr Agrawal they gave a general update on the work in the palace. There were three separate teams, with Mac in overall charge, so Priya presumed her presence was required, while the other team leaders weren't, because they would discuss the scoping work. Instead, when Mr Agrawal asked for the initial assessment now they'd completed the site visits he directed his question at Mac.

Mac answered, in a way which suggested he'd been supervising her scoping work much closer than he had in reality. She didn't mind. It was better than being the centre of attention where she was most likely to slip up and make a bad impression.

They were briefly interrupted when Mr Agrawal took a phone call. He spoke in Adsahi but from his tone he was excited and she could understand him saying 'of course' and 'definitely'.

After the call, Mr Agrawal looked expectantly at the door. Moments later, Rohan strode in.

Priya's heart began to pound. She hadn't seen him since their conversation over omelettes. He was dressed casually in a cotton shirt with the sleeves rolled up. She remembered being in the embrace of those sinewy forearms. She cleared her throat and turned her attention to Mr Agrawal. That was safer for her thoughts.

'Sorry I interrupted,' Rohan said.

'Not at all, Yuvaraja-sahib. Mr MacFarlane was finishing an update on the scoping exercise.'

'Mr MacFarlane was?' Rohan raised, his eyebrows looking between Mr Agrawal, Mac and her. 'Ms Sen has been doing the site visits. Wouldn't it be better to get the update directly from her?'

Priya threw a worried glance at Mac. He knew Rohan had accompanied her on some of the site visits, but Mac might not like Rohan going round his authority to her for a report.

She waited a moment in case Mac was going to reply. When he made no sign he intended to speak, she spoke looking down at her lap. 'Oh, I update Mac regularly. He knows everything I do, Ro… Yuvaraja-sahib. His report to Mr Agrawal is comprehensive.' She quickly looked at Mac again, hoping she'd said the right thing, but he was looking at Rohan.

'Then please go on, Mac,' Rohan said.

While Mac repeated his report, Priya took a chance to surreptitiously peek from under her eyelashes at Rohan, expecting his attention to be on Mac. But Rohan was looking directly at her. His expression was contemplative.

She hastily dropped her eyes. Why was Rohan looking at her like that? She replayed the scene since he came into the office quickly in her mind. Rohan had, probably unknowingly, given her the opportunity to showcase her expertise and passion for the project. And she'd blown it. Self-doubt had overridden her desire, her dream, to lead this work and she let her manager speak for her instead.

After hearing the report and asking questions, which Mac was able to answer because of the comprehensive briefings she gave him every day, Rohan left the room. Mr Agrawal and Mac wanted to discuss another potential scheme on restoring the paintings in some government buildings. Since restoration wasn't Priya's area of expertise, she took her leave of them.

She had barely walked a few steps when Rohan called her name. She turned and saw him coming out of the shadows. Although he'd left through the door leading to the royal corridor he was now in a staff corridor.

Did it mean he purposely waited to see her? Her heart began to race. But she forced herself to think rationally. They had shared a kiss. An out-of-this-world, never-to-be-forgotten kiss, but Rohan had made it clear it was a one-off.

She waited patiently for him to speak. After the silence stretched out she said, 'Can I help you with something, Yuvaraja-sahib?'

'Um…how is everything with the site visits?' he asked.

Priya furrowed her brow. He'd just received an extensive update on the subject. 'I may be able to have the report with you earlier than I expected.'

He nodded. 'Excellent. Is the work on the palace murals progressing faster than expected then?'

'Yes, but I've been given a few days leave over the weekend. I'm going to work on the report then.'

'If you're on leave, shouldn't you rest and relax?'

'I'll do some relaxing—maybe tour the island. I would love to see cave six again. If it would be all right, even if it's not for a site visit.'

'I have no problem with it. But why don't you go to mainland India? Lots more to see there. I can ask my assistant to help you with any arrangements.'

'Thank you, sir. That isn't necessary. I'm happy to stay around here.'

'It's going to be chaos around here from now on,' Rohan said with a grin. 'If you think the preparations have been hectic so far, they're about to enter warp speed with the gala so close. Not only in the palace but over the whole of Adysara too. Believe me, you don't want to be here if you don't have to be. Take my advice and escape while you can. You'll thank me.'

They laughed. 'I'll think about it.'

Laughter fled as they continued to gaze into each other's eyes. Desire clear in them.

'Priya,' he whispered, coming to stand closer to her. 'I... I...'

Priya waited for him to close the gap between them, for him to take her in his arms and cover his mouth with hers.

'Yes,' she breathed back.

'I have to go.' He stepped away, squeezed her shoulder then turned towards the royal quarters.

She stared after him. What an impossible situation. Why did she have to fall for a prince?

CHAPTER TEN

OVER BREAKFAST THE next morning, Rohan listened to his mother as she updated the family on the final arrangements for the gala. He could feel the tension as she spoke, since, although this wasn't the first gala she'd overseen since becoming the Maharani, it was going to be a landmark one. If she'd constructed the perfect guest list, Rohan would meet the woman he would one day marry.

Although his mind accepted the factual reality, his heart rebelled against it.

He'd always accepted his role, his duty was to this island and the people on it; he was usually happy and eager to do what was expected of him. Adysara needed economic growth; without it his country would decline and the way to avoid that was by marrying someone who could help bring investment to the island, directly or indirectly. He knew he didn't have the freedom to choose his life partner in the way some others did. It had never been a problem. His parents had grown to love each other and Rohan always believed he would grow to love the woman he married, in so much as love existed at all. But over the last few weeks, for the first time in his life, he wished it could be different and the idea of marrying someone he didn't know became less appealing.

Not that his parents were expecting him to marry a stranger. The intention was to invite a few select guests to stay at the palace for a few days after the gala. It was an unspoken tradition that many families with marriage-able females would be hoping for an invitation for after the festivities. He would get to know the women better, without hundreds of people watching their every move.

At her request, he accompanied his mother as they inspected the rooms which had al-ready been prepared. There was an aura of ex-citement among the palace workers, over and above the usual excitement for a gala. Every-one knew this particular gala was a prelude to a greater occasion—his wedding.

Suddenly the bustle around him felt oppres-sive. As soon as he could, without drawing unnecessary attention, he excused himself and went straight to his suite of rooms. But the walls seemed to close in on him there too. Needing fresh air, he walked onto the balcony.

He needed to get away. Out of the palace. Off the island.

He'd suggested Priya go to the mainland for a few days. Perhaps he should follow his own advice. Since Priya also had some time off, it would make sense if they travelled together. Taking his plane would be more convenient for her than her taking the ferry across to the mainland. He could act as her tour guide.

Was it a bad idea to spend more time with Priya when, despite his best intentions, his mind involuntarily replayed their kiss on a regular loop? They had already discussed their mutual attraction and agreed they wouldn't act on it again. Priya knew he couldn't offer her a brief relationship, she understood there was no future for them.

Did it mean he had to stay away from her? He'd already done that over the past few days, not going on the site visits with her. He hadn't expected to see her in Govinda Agrawal's office yesterday evening.

They way her face had lit up when she first saw him before she pulled herself back and gave him a polite smile. The polite smile meant she wasn't comfortable in the situation. The polite smile meant she wasn't thinking of him as Rohan but as Mr Varma, or worse Yuvaraja.

He disliked that polite smile intensely.

Before they'd given in to their attraction and shared their explosive kiss, she was relaxed in his company. Could they go back to an easy-going friendship if they spent more time together rather than less?

Could he honestly ignore his attraction to her?

It would be difficult. Last night, when it was the two of them alone in the shadows, he'd almost given in to temptation and kissed her again.

But he hadn't. He'd overridden his impulse and stepped away. That was a good sign. He'd rather have Priya as a friend than avoid her because he desired her.

The only problem with his decision to go to the mainland was Priya hadn't sounded eager to take the time off, so would she come away? Rohan replayed some of their previous conversations, trying to come up with an incentive.

Moments later, an idea came to him. He sent her a message and asked her to meet him in his private gardens after she'd finished work. It would be the perfect place to talk. It was a short distance from the palace so it wasn't overlooked. And it was walled with a single door which was kept locked so nobody else had access to it unless he wanted them to.

It used to be his grandmother's place. She wanted an area which she could tend herself— planting her own flowers and vegetables. A small oasis where she could throw off the trappings of royalty. After she passed away, his father gave the garden to him.

And he wanted Priya to see it.

Walking to his desk, he clapped his hands together ready to put his plans into action. Once seated he paused. He wasn't going to demand Priya accompany him. And she might, she probably would, have some ideas for how to spend her weekend. He would put his plane on standby for the following morning but otherwise he wasn't going to assume she'd automatically fall in with his plans just because he wanted her too.

But he couldn't wait to tell her what he had in mind.

Hours later he was in his garden. He'd rushed through his work with an eagerness which had been missing since he arrived back at the palace. All because of his desire to have a clear plate to go away for the weekend. He would be going regardless of whether Priya wanted to come with him.

His parents had been understanding when he told them his intention. Almost sympathetic. His father had already gone through the same experience so he probably had an idea of how Rohan was feeling.

Rohan glanced at his watch. He'd been waiting in his private garden for ten minutes—he hoped Priya was going to turn up. He'd sent her directions, but what if they weren't clear enough and she was wandering through the vast grounds of the palace looking for him. He would need to organise a search party unless someone in her team was able to track her.

He should have asked her to share her location with him. He laughed as the thought crossed his mind. That was too close to stalker behaviour.

Priya was probably fine. She was simply running a little late. His wasn't so high and mighty as a royal he couldn't wait a few minutes for someone.

'Sorry, sorry,' Priya called as she rushed through the door. 'It took longer to finish things because Mac is still insisting I take the long weekend.' She smiled, then slowly did a three-hundred-and-sixty-degree turn.

'This place is beautiful. I haven't seen some of the trees anywhere before.'

'It's become a little wild,' Rohan admitted. 'The trees come from different parts of the island, but they were cultivated to grow in this garden. There's a bench over here. Why don't we sit down so we can talk?'

'Of course,' she replied, following him. But he could see her eyes dart around the garden trying to take everything in.

'Do you like gardening?' he asked.

She shrugged. 'Don't know. Never had a garden.'

'Never?'

'Well, we had a small garden when my mum was alive. But I was too young to have much to do with it at the time. Then it was boarding school. And mine didn't have a gardening club or anything. Now I live on the third floor of a block of flats. But one day, I'm going to buy a house with a garden.'

It was such a simple goal. One he could help her achieve with the click of his fingers—there were plenty of lovely homes with gardens on Adysara. What other goals and dreams did she have? He wanted to make every dream of hers come true.

'I think we should go away together this weekend,' he blurted out.

She whipped round to face him. 'Pardon?'

'I want to get away from the palace for a few days. I thought it would be a good opportunity to visit Ajanta and Ellora—tour the caves, examine how the sites have been preserved and generate some ideas which we can implement here. Since you've got a few days off too, I thought you might want to come along.'

He held his breath, waiting for her response. Would the caves at Ajanta and Ellora be enough of an inducement? He thought it was perfect. He hadn't visited them in years and he knew Priya had never visited them.

'Ajanta and Ellora?' she repeated. 'You're going to see them this weekend?'

'Yes.'

'And I can come too?'

'If you want.'

'What about transport and accommodation? Won't it be too short notice to arrange those?'

'No,' he answered emphatically. He liked that she forgot he was royalty most of the time. He could go about almost incognito when he was off the island, but his status had its advantages—such as having a private plane at his disposal and hotel suites whenever he needed them.

'Are you sure it's a good idea for us to go together?' she asked, unable to maintain eye contact.

'Why not?'

'I thought you were avoiding me.'

He laughed to cover his guilt. 'No, I've just been busy.'

'Of course. Of course, you've been busy. You're the prince. I was silly thinking you were avoiding me because I kissed you.'

'We'll have to agree to disagree on who kissed whom since you insist on taking the blame. But there's no reason for us to avoid each other is there? We already discussed this. I can't offer you a real relationship. A real romantic relationship. But we can be friends, can't we?'

She swallowed—he could tell her mind was whirring a mile a minute. 'I'd like that,' she said.

He hadn't realised he was holding his breath for her response until he felt an overwhelming sense of relief.

An alarm went off.

'I'm going to have to go back soon,' he said. 'They've organised a dance tutor to show me some of the formal dances. Nightmare. But it'll be worth it if you save a dance for me so I can show you what I've learned.'

'A dance?' her tone making her astonishment obvious.

'At the gala ball.'

'The gala?' She snorted. 'I'm not going to be at the gala, Rohan. I work here. I'm not a guest.'

He paused, the thought she wasn't going to the dance never occurring to him before. She was right. She wasn't a dignitary. She didn't have a wealthy family. She wasn't invited to the event that was consuming every waking moment of the people around him.

Instead she'd be going to the celebrations in town. And he would be whisking some stranger round the dance floor.

He didn't know what to say, but if the reminder of the difference in their situation was bothering her, she didn't show it.

Instead she grinned and bit her bottom lip. He groaned wishing he could run his tongue across the impressions her teeth had left. He worked hard to concentrate on what she was saying.

'I can't believe I'm going to see Ajanta and Ellora. It's like all my dreams are coming true.'

She carried on telling him everything she knew about the caves and in what ways they were similar to the caves on Adysara—her face animated and flushed with the passion for her subject.

He also had a dream, one which he'd been having since he got to know Priya. But it was one which none of the advantages of being a prince could ever make come true. In fact his royal status meant the opposite.

CHAPTER ELEVEN

PRIYA WOKE UP with the dawn on Saturday morning. She still couldn't believe she would be seeing the caves at Ajanta today. They were planning an early start since it was still a three-hour drive from the hotel.

After a quick shower and freshening up, Priya got changed into a lightweight pink cotton T-shirt and beige linen trousers and put a headscarf into her bag. From everything she'd read, it could be very hot walking between the caves although the interior of the caves would be cool.

Once she was ready, she walked out of her room into the living area of the suite she was sharing with Rohan. A breakfast of cut fruit, poori bhaji, stuffed paratha, lassi, fruit juice and coffees and teas had already been laid out for them. She would never get used to this level of opulence. She was still recovering from flying in a private plane, which as a

luxury in itself, meant they could fly directly
to the airport at Aurangabad.

On the flight, Rohan told her his assistant
had booked a two-bedroom suite, with the assumption it would be more practical for meals
and discussing work. But Rohan offered to
arrange a separate hotel room for her if she
preferred.

She'd told him it wasn't necessary. His assistant was correct that sharing a suite would
be practical. It had been an easy decision to
make.

They'd already had a frank discussion
about their attraction, a couple of times now.
There was something special about knowing
he wanted her as much as she wanted him—
she'd never experienced that before—even if
they couldn't be together. And she accepted
that, with his bride-finding gala coming up,
he couldn't even offer her a brief relationship.
She wasn't naive enough to think it would be
easy, her attraction to him wasn't going away
all of a sudden. It was something she could
keep in check. And she wasn't going to turn
down the opportunity of spending time in
his company.

The previous evening, they'd checked into
their rooms by early afternoon so they decided to take a visit to Panchakki, the water

mill complex which offered scenic views of Aurangabad. It had gone well—they were relaxed and at ease with each other.

'Morning,' Rohan said as he walked into the room. Priya couldn't help noticing how wide his chest was as he stretched. 'Did you sleep well?'

'Very well thanks. I think all the walking and fresh air helped. How about you?'

'Good, thanks. Hopefully you'll have a similar sleep tonight after walking around the caves.'

She nodded. Hopefully not. It was partially the truth she'd slept well. She'd fallen asleep quickly but her dreams featured Rohan heavily and she woke during the night massively aroused and aching for him.

Over breakfast they discussed which of the thirty caves they definitely wanted to see on their tour. Rohan had arranged a private guide to meet them at Ajanta to show them around.

A few minutes later, the hotel phone buzzed. Rohan answered it.

'The car's waiting for us,' he said.

The journey to the caves went by quickly. The car dropped them at a viewing point, before they reached the caves' entrance, then went to park.

From where they stood, Priya and Rohan

were able to get a panoramic view of the basalt rock-cut caves carved out of a vertical cliff.

'Wow!' Priya expelled a reverent breath. 'Can you believe we're standing in front of structures crafted in first century BCE? How in the world did they have the tools to create something so perfect?'

She took out her camera to capture the vista before her. Then she turned and walked up to Rohan. 'Thank you. Thank you for bringing me here.' It was such a thoughtful, caring gesture from Rohan to invite her. He could have gone anywhere for his weekend away but he'd picked a place which he knew she'd dreamed of visiting. A cautionary voice in her head was telling her to stop, but she ignored it, giving in to the impulse to throw her arms around Rohan.

'You are most welcome,' he replied, returning her hug and resting his cheek on the top of her head. She felt the whisper of a kiss on her hair before he pulled away. 'The guide will be waiting for us.'

For the next few hours, they wandered around the vihara and worship halls, examining the painting which narrated the Jataka tales.

Outside cave sixteen, she grabbed Rohan's hand to point out the palace scene fresco, very similar to ones in the caves on Adysara. When they moved on to the next relief, neither had let go.

Priya reassured herself she was a sensible woman. They admitted they fancied each other. But she hadn't admitted her feelings or touched on the emotional connection she felt with Rohan. She wasn't ready to explore those feelings too deeply, her protective instincts kicking in. It had been safer to focus on the physical.

She always tried to ground herself in reality but standing in the Ajanta caves she'd always wanted to visit, her hand safe in the strong hand of the handsome, intelligent, thoughtful man next to her, for a moment she indulged in a flight of fancy where she could make believe they were simply a couple, enjoying a tour round a place with a beautiful history. For a moment she could make believe she wasn't plain Priya Sen of nowhere from nobody; and he wasn't Rohan Varma, Yuvaraja of Adysara. For a moment she could make believe he could be hers.

But reality, in the form of their tour guide, called her back. She pulled her hand from Rohan's, noticing how he tried to hold on a little longer. She flexed her hand—now empty and cold.

Was it a mistake coming away with him if she couldn't control herself in his company? She stared at the statue in front of her. If she couldn't pull herself together, she was going to waste the opportunity of a lifetime having a guided tour of Ajanta's wonders.

She took a few moments to compose herself and adopt her professional persona. No more thinking about Rohan. No more thinking about things that couldn't be.

Priya was exhausted when they finally left Ajanta, falling asleep in the car back to the hotel. After a quick stop in their room to freshen up, they decided to take a taxi into the town to look for somewhere to eat.

After their dinner, they went to Bibi Ka Maqbara.

As she stood next to a pillar, viewing the mausoleum with its resemblance to the Taj Mahal, she thought about the story of Shah Jahan's monument to his lost love.

She would never regret this weekend and being with someone who made it clear he liked her and enjoyed her company. He would never know how rare that was for her. So if the mistake wasn't coming away with Rohan, what if the mistake would be not acting on their attraction? If only for the weekend.

She glanced at Rohan through the corner of her eyes. He was looking at the same view, but occasionally he looked in her direction with an enigmatic smile.

Priya had never been the kind of person who put herself forward. She tried not to stick her head over the precipice. And sometimes it meant she waited for things to happen. She was always hoping people would notice her— previous boyfriends, employers, her father. But waiting never got her anywhere.

She was with Rohan; a man she liked and wanted, who didn't hide that he liked and wanted her too. She wasn't naive. He had a duty to his family and his country and his people. She understood duty better than many people.

So what if they couldn't have for ever? So what if they couldn't have weeks or months?

What if a few hours was enough?

This was one of the scariest things she would ever do, but she was going to do it. She was going to claim a brief moment for something she desperately wanted.

She stepped away from the pillar, walked over to Rohan, and slipped her hand into his.

It was the biggest, loudest gesture she'd ever made.

Priya's hand fit perfectly in his own. He'd almost stopped breathing when he'd felt the first warm touch of her palm, before her fingers entwined with his.

What did their clasped hands mean?

He'd been clear he couldn't offer her a relationship of any kind. She'd accepted that and, knowing her as he did, she wasn't the kind of person to try persuading him to change his mind. But something was different.

He wanted to know what she was thinking, but it wasn't a conversation they should have in public. The temptation to hurry Priya through Bibi Ka Maqbara was strong. She laughed and chatted as easily as the other times on their site visits, before they'd kissed. But there was something more between them now. Although the surface level of their conversation was about their visits, there was also a subtext in the looks she gave him from under lowered eyelids, in the light caresses on his arm as she walked past him, in the slow, seductive smiles she gave him when he glanced her way.

Was it his imagination or was she moving faster than before?

He hailed a taxi and they were soon on the way back to the hotel. The tension in the car was electric, both of them staring straight ahead, not looking at each other, as if they knew they couldn't control themselves if they did.

He had no expectations. Yes, of course, he hoped the looks and gestures meant Priya wanted something to happen between them that evening. But if holding hands and secret smiles were all they would share, it would be enough for him. He would take whatever she offered.

He turned to look out of the car window. And if she did want to make love with him, would one weekend really be enough? Did it matter? It had to be enough. He wasn't free to love someone totally of his own choosing. He'd always known his duty was to improve the quality of life for the people of Adysara by any means possible, including his choice of wife. And he wouldn't change that. Even if he knew how.

As they got closer to the hotel, Priya looked in his direction, her lips parting as she ran her tongue across them. He groaned. This was torture.

As soon as the car stopped, he rushed out, not waiting for the hotel doorman to open the door for them. Holding hands, they entered the hotel, walking straight through the foyer to the private lift that would take them to the suite. The moment the lift doors closed, he turned to her. They both took a step forward.

'Priya,' he groaned.

She stretched her arms around his neck, pulling his head closer to hers, as his arm enveloped her waist, drawing her to his body until there wasn't a centimetre between them. His mouth covered hers, devouring all the sweetness she had to offer.

He lifted her so her feet were off the floor and carried her to the door of the suite, never breaking contact with her lips. He fumbled with the key card like a teenager on the night of the prom, desperate to get inside. Priya wasn't making it any easier, meeting kiss after kiss, barely taking a breath, wrapping her legs around his waist.

He swore as he still couldn't get the door open. Priya giggled and shimmied out of his arms, back onto the floor, taking the card out of his hands. The door opened on her first attempt.

The lamps in the room were casting a low

light. The curtains were still open but the view wasn't of interest right then.

The door had barely closed behind them when they were reaching for each other, as if the only place they could imagine being in this moment was in each other's arms. He couldn't believe how lucky he was to have this woman he'd desired from the first moment he'd seen her returning the passion of his kisses with equal ferocity.

He inhaled sharply when he felt her hands creep under his shirt, tracing the outline of his abdominal muscles. Before he threw all caution to the wind he had to make sure they knew exactly where they stood. With a Herculean effort, he removed his mouth from hers.

Her lips were swollen, her cheeks flushed, her hair mussed from where he'd run his fingers through.

'Priya, Priya,' he whispered, dotting kisses over every inch of her face. 'You are so beautiful. Perfect. Are you sure this is what you want?'

'Yes.' Her answer was simple. Sincere.

'You know this is all I can offer, this short fling. I can't offer you a future.' He punctuated each word with a kiss.

'I know. I understand. I'm not asking for

more. But we can have this weekend. That will be enough.'

Rohan swept a curl behind Priya's ear, resting his forehead against hers, trying to calm the maelstrom within him. Would it be enough, he thought again. He wasn't sure it would be for him. But it was all he could offer, and it was what she was willing to accept. He was too selfish to do the, probably, honourable thing and walk away.

His hand moved under her top and eased a bra cup to the side. A moan of pleasure escaped Priya's lips as he lightly skimmed his fingers over her curves. Hastily she undid his shirt buttons, splaying her hand across his chest, before moving lower.

Trousers and pants caught at his feet. He hadn't stopped to take his shoes off. He kicked them behind him with a clumsy haste, not wanting to break contact with Priya in case this turned out to be another one of his sensual dreams.

'I have condoms in my bathroom,' he said as he unbuttoned Priya's trousers. He couldn't wait until he had her under him on his bed.

'I have some in my bag,' she said twisting round to look for it.

She bent over to pick up her bag and take out a pouch. He groaned. They weren't going to make it to the bed.

* * *

Priya woke up before the alarm the next morning. She snuggled back under the blanket, reluctant to leave the warmth. Her eyelids refused to lift—she felt like she'd barely slept. Which was true.

As if they didn't want to waste a single second of their time together, they talked and made love until finally succumbing to sleep just before dawn.

'Good morning,' a voiced rasped in her ear before Rohan's lips moved to nuzzle into her neck, tightening his arm around her waist.

'Morning.' She turned onto her back, reaching round his neck to pull him in for a kiss. 'We should get up soon. We want to get to Ellora as soon as it opens.'

Rohan murmured, bending to press light kisses from her mouth down her neck to her breasts. 'Do we?' he asked, looking into her eyes as his hands captured the places his mouth had just been.

Heat flared. Did they have to visit Ellora? Wouldn't the caves be the same as Ajanta's?

Amused by how tempted she was to blow off a visit to a heritage site she'd wanted to visit since she first heard about it, she made a big effort to throw the covers off them. The air conditioning in the room was not quite as effective as a cold shower, but it was enough for Rohan to roll off her with a groan of protest.

'Fine. I promised you a trip to the caves and I will deliver. Why don't you get ready while I'll arrange for breakfast? Or I could you join you in the shower?' he suggested with a lift of his eyebrows.

'You know if you do that we won't leave for hours,' Priya replied, forcing herself to get out of bed.

He shrugged. 'Spoil-sport.'

Priya laughed, throwing the first thing that came to hand at him. Unfortunately it was her panties.

'Not helping,' Rohan said, holding them up, as if taunting her to take them from him, which would involve her climbing onto him.

She shook her head. She wasn't risking that. 'Come on, no dawdling. Have patience. We have tonight.'

Rohan's face froze. She'd meant to tease him with the promise of later. Instead she could only think how the night would be the last time they could be together like this. Once they got back to Adysara, life would go on as before.

As Priya got ready for the day she considered her options. She could waste their precious little time together, whining and complaining about how just how little that time was. And why do that when there was no guarantee this attraction, this desire they felt for each other would last beyond a few days anyway.

Or she could make the most of every second she had, touring round the beautiful caves of Ellora with a gorgeous man by her side, then spending the night back in this hotel making love to him until dawn.

CHAPTER TWELVE

'HEY PRIYA,' Mac greeted her. 'I didn't see you at breakfast this morning. I wasn't sure whether you were back. I was hoping perhaps you'd taken my advice and extended your break.' He was referring to a message he'd sent her while she was away.

Priya tried to smile, but her lips barely moved upwards. 'I came back last night, it was later than planned, so I went straight to sleep. I skipped breakfast because I wanted to check everything was ready for our work today.'

She hadn't been able to sleep anyway. She needed to keep busy. Her weekend with Rohan had been sublime but on Monday evening, as she and Rohan had approached the airstrip on Adysara, the space between them had increased, literally and figuratively. Priya wouldn't regret, couldn't regret spending the weekend with Rohan; it had been the most magical time she had ever experienced. But it was never real. Reality had been nipping at her heels for too long and she couldn't ignore it any more.

She'd spent two perfect nights in his arms. Now, whatever it had been, it was over.

She needed to concentrate on her job. She couldn't expect Rohan to offer her a future—he'd been very clear on that. And who was she to ask him to change his mind?

Priya and Mac had a quick chat about her trip—swapping their impressions of the different sculptures and wall paintings at Ajanta and Ellora. She still needed to finish her report and then Mac would probably want to visits the caves and murals before they submitted the report to the palace, but they had some enforced time away from work coming up where they could fit it in.

In the four days she and Rohan had been gone, the preparations for the gala had advanced at a hectic pace. Most of the rooms, which would be used for the events, were decorated and cleared of all evidence of the hordes of people who had passed through getting them ready.

There was still two and a half weeks until the first event, and her team wasn't expected to finish all the mural restorations before the gala, since they were working in an area that would be closed off to the guests. But they would be expected to cordon off the mural and leave the area cleared of their tools by then. None of the restoration team would be doing anyway work in the palace for the duration of the gala.

Six days without any work to do. She didn't need the time off since she has just taken the long weekend, but she wasn't going to be given any choice in the matter. Again. While the gala was on, she would be spending time with her co-workers, touring the island and taking part in the festivities organised for the islanders.

For the next few hours, Priya was able to throw herself into her work. Her team was excellent. She would love to continue working with them on this project but she had overheard someone saying Leo Blake's family situation was under control and he was available to return.

Mac hadn't mentioned anything to her. Perhaps if she kept her head down, buried in the sand, she could stay on Adysara. She would go wherever the company sent her, but she couldn't imagine any other project offering anything like the artwork on Adysara.

Her job was all she had left. She had no

family to speak of, no partner—her fling with
Rohan was a moment out of time.

For the next few days, before the gala hia-
tus, she would try to show how capable and
indispensable she was. They didn't need to
go to the trouble of asking Leo Blake to return. Would it be enough? Would she be able
to show Mac, Mr Agrawal and Rohan she was
good enough to carry on leading this project,
and perhaps the larger project that was potentially her company's for the asking?

It was only when her team members started
packing away their tools that she realised it
was the end of the working day. She stretched
and eased out the kinks in her back and neck.
Tempted as she was to continue, Priya knew
the light would soon fade until its quality
wasn't suitable to do the detailed technical
work.

She hadn't joined the others for a lunch
break and now her stomach was rumbling.
It was still a couple of hours before dinner
would be served. She went to the break room
hoping there would be some fruit or snacks
left out. Unfortunately, there wasn't.

Instead she headed back to her quarters
to cook something for herself. All she could
find in the kitchen was some bread, eggs and
onions.

Immediately, her mind went back to the day Rohan had cooked an omelette for her. She grunted out of frustration. Why was it the second she didn't have physical tasks to occupy her, her thoughts went straight to Rohan? It was the reason she'd avoided taking a lunch break.

She was physically attracted to him and now she had slept with him. It should have been enough to scratch that itch. It wasn't and she knew it wouldn't be. It didn't alter the fact it was all she could have. The sooner she accepted it and didn't hope or wish for the impossible she would be able to move on.

Love, marriage, children weren't in her future. And if she didn't know this already, it would never be—could never be—with Rohan.

Not for the first time, she wished her mother was there to confide in. There was no point wishing she could talk to her father or stepmother. She already knew they weren't interested in anything she did.

How could someone who wasn't loved by her family, the people who were supposed to love her most, ever expect a prince to care about her?

After dinner, instead of joining the rest of the team in the lounge, she would spend her evening working on her report. The sooner she finished it, the sooner she could hand it over. From now until the end of the project she needed to reduce the chance of meeting with Rohan again.

She opened her laptop and was pulling up her report when her phone pinged. Not her personal phone, the phone Rohan gave her, with a message asking her to meet him in his private garden in half an hour.

She'd just given herself a lecture on getting used to being alone, on the necessity, for the sake of her heart, to avoid coming into contact with Rohan. All he'd had to do was send her a text and those sensible decisions evaporated faster than a snowflake would in Adysara's heat. He was still the royal family member with the interest in the preservation and con-servation work, she rationalised. Maybe he wanted to speak to her about their project and the ideas they'd had when they toured Ajanta and Ellora. And maybe he wanted to meet in the garden because he needed the fresh air.

Whatever the reason, she couldn't give up the chance to see him again.

Half an hour later, she was on her way to Rohan's private garden despite her instincts screaming it was a bad idea. Whenever she was in Rohan's company, her libido threatened to override her common sense.

She'd already replied to his message saying she would meet him; she couldn't really change her mind. But it was time to behave sensibly again.

Now they were back on the island, the same rules from before their weekend applied. She was part of a project team and he was the crown prince. They weren't going to have clandestine meetings in the garden.

In fact, the best option would be if they kept their meetings to a minimum—only about work and, preferably, never alone. Priya didn't know why Rohan asked to see her but she hoped he was thinking along the same lines. She would make her view clear if it wasn't the reason he wanted to meet.

He was already in the garden, pacing back and forth by the bench. She stood at the entrance, watching his powerful strides. He glanced at his watch then looked towards the entrance.

Her heart flipped at the way his face lit up. He never tried to hide how happy he was to see her. Despite her determination, only seconds earlier, when Rohan ran over to her and swept her off her feet, she met his kiss passionately.

'Hey,' he said, when they finally broke apart.

'Hey.'

'How was your day?' His mouth moved over her hairline.

'Good. Busy. Making good progress. How was yours?'

'Busy. I spent all day in meetings going through protocols for our guests and running through where I have to stand and when,' he said, punctuating his words with kisses to her cheeks, her eyelids, her brows and finally her lips again.

Caught up in the haze of desire, it took a while for his reminder that the gala was more than a big party for him to penetrate her consciousness. It should have been enough to stop their embrace but Priya didn't want to let go.

'No regrets about the weekend?' Rohan asked, when they finally stopped kissing.

'None. What about you?'

'Only that it couldn't have been for longer.'

A warm glow flowed through her at his admission. If only they'd met months or even years before so they could have spent real time together before his responsibilities inevitably pulled them apart. It didn't seem fair that the weekend was all they could have.

'But it can't be,' she said, taking a few steps away. 'We knew that.'

He walked up to her, taking her hand to lead her to a bench where he pulled her onto his lap. 'Let's not talk about it now. I've been waiting to see you all day.'

The next minutes were spent with little talking and lots of long, drugging kisses and caresses until they were panting and dishevelled. Priya got off Rohan's lap and sat next to him to put herself back in order.

'Will you meet me tomorrow, same time?' he asked.

She almost laughed from pure delight at the realisation he couldn't bear to say goodbye. After so many years, and bad relationships where she'd felt unloved and uncared for, it was a heady feeling to be wanted by such a caring, thoughtful, gorgeous man.

'Is that possible?' she asked, eagerly. 'Isn't your time going to be spent getting ready for the gala, greeting your guests. I heard some of them have started to arrive already.'

'Some guests from the States,' he admitted. 'I haven't met them yet, but I'll meet them over dinner. But it doesn't mean I can't spend time with you.'

Priya hesitated. Was continuing to meet

Rohan wise when he would be meeting potential brides in a few days?'

'Priya, I'm not promised to anyone yet. We
aren't doing anything wrong by meeting here.
We're not hurting anyone.'

Priya wasn't sure it was entirely true. She
suspected the way she was feeling was going
to lead to a whole load of hurt for her soon.

But she could deal with that afterwards.
She'd have the rest of her life to deal with
it. For now, she was going to grab on to a
small sliver of happiness with Rohan while
she could.

CHAPTER THIRTEEN

ROHAN STOOD ERECT, dressed in his official regalia, behind his father's throne. He was at the first official event for the gala celebration—the formal receiving of the guests.

Each family would walk up the long, carpeted aisle, make their pranam or bow, receive a nod from his father and a smile from his mother before moving off to the side to watch the next family enter.

It was old-fashioned. It was pomp and circumstance. It was slightly ridiculous but it was tradition.

He'd already met most of the guests, informally, as they arrived over the past week. There were several eligible women present, but he'd been careful about how much time he spent in their company.

Everybody knew this year's gala was also where he would be looking for his future wife. If he gave one particular woman more attention than any of the others, he could risk gossip and speculation. Since he had no intention of carefully calculating how long he spent with someone and making sure he spent the same amount of time with everyone else, it was easier if he restricted himself to only meeting when everyone was together.

At least that's what he told himself. If he was being completely honest, there was only one woman who he wanted to spend time with. And she wasn't even allowed in the palace at the moment.

Since they'd returned from Aurungabad, they'd met every evening after work in his garden. He wanted to cover her with kisses, with his body and make love to her over and over. But he knew he had to maintain some distance so he restricted himself to holding her in his arms. And they talked. And it had to be enough.

As soon as he was finished with the reception line, he went to his room to change out of his uniform. He tried to be patient as his staff helped him remove the regalia and handle it careful when he really wanted to fling it off him and get to the garden as soon as possible. From tomorrow, the festivities would begin in earnest and he wouldn't have the time to leave the palace. Who knew when he would get the chance to see Priya alone again?

He was sure his family knew where he was going in the evenings, and he had to tell his assistant where he would be for security purposes—but once they were in the garden and closed the door, the walls provided a sanctuary. As if the walls were keeping the secret of his relationship with Priya.

She smiled when she saw him, walking over to greet him with a hug. Although he knew he shouldn't, the realisation this could be the last time he was holding her made him hold on tighter, lowering his head and lifting her mouth to his.

She didn't push him away, meeting his kisses with a reciprocal passion.

He held her away from him slightly, drinking her in, committing her form to his memory. She looked so beautiful and serene in the moonlight. She would make an incredible queen. It wasn't fair he wasn't free to choose her.

CHAPTER FOURTEEN

TWO DAYS LATER, it was the night of the gala ball and Priya was in the town centre with the rest of her company, watching the dance performance which was part of the celebrations which had been put on for the islanders and other people who weren't attending the ball itself.

They'd already had a long and lavish meal which had been arranged on behalf of the royal family. She could understand how all the islanders looked forward to this gala week, and this evening in particular. The atmosphere was relaxed, fun, informal. She wondered whether the people at the palace were having as much fun. Ever since Rohan had mentioned his dance tutor, in her imagination, the ball was like a scene from a Regency film with groups of dancers moving in formation to set pieces.

What would Rohan be doing? He must have

been spending time with all his guests, with the large number of women who had come to Adysara knowing Rohan was looking for a queen. Perhaps at that moment he was dancing with the woman who would be his future bride.

'This is amazing,' one of her co-workers said. 'They really know how to throw a party.'

'Think what the actual gala is like if this is the non-official one,' another co-worker replied. 'Think about what the wedding festivities will be like. I hope I'm still working here when it happens.'

'We probably will be here,' the first speaker said. 'I heard the wedding usually happens within eighteen months of this event. Priya, do you think we'll still be working here?'

Priya forced her mouth to smile. 'It's a long project,' she replied, although a hollow pit had formed in her stomach.

How had she failed to realise the next big celebration on the island would be Rohan's wedding. If she continued working on the preservation and conservation of the stonework on Adysara then she could still be on the island when he got married. She would have to watch it happen.

The idea was devastating.

She'd always understood Rohan couldn't

offer her a future. He'd been clear about that and she'd been under no illusions. It wasn't something she could protest against, even if she was the kind of person who kicked up a fuss. It was simply a fact. It was what it was.

But it was one thing to know on an intellectual level Rohan couldn't be hers and another to actually see him married to someone else, out of her reach for ever.

She stumbled back as if she'd been punched in the gut.

This reaction wasn't the kind she would have if this was simply a short-lived love affair coming to an end. The pain she was reeling from was worse than when any of her former boyfriends, men she believed she was in love with, ended things with her.

She needed time and space, and quiet, to process what her reaction meant. She should head back to her room. There was too much activity here, too much noise, it was too full of life. She needed to be alone.

Her phone vibrated—the phone Rohan had given her. She wished she had the strength to ignore it, but she took it out of her handbag and read the message from Rohan asking him to meet her in the garden.

She frowned. The last time they'd met, he'd told her he wouldn't be able to come to the garden while the gala festivities were taking place. Although he hadn't specifically said so, she assumed from that point on the only times she would see him would be on a professional basis because he would have surely met and narrowed down his choice of potential brides and would be expected to entertain them.

Why, then, was he asking her to meet him? Was something wrong?

But a rational part of her knew by now this behaviour was par for the course for them. So many times they'd made agreements they weren't able to stick to—first they'd agreed there could be no relationship between them, then they'd agreed it would be a short weekend fling and everything would be back to normal when they were back in Adysara, afterward they'd agreed they would only meet until the gala festivities began, but they hadn't kept to that agreement either.

Rohan constantly showed her how much he liked spending time with her. It was almost as if he wasn't ready to say it was over.

Priya felt a heaviness in her chest. Soon what they wanted wouldn't matter. Rohan didn't have a choice in his future. He would have to marry for the good of Adysara. Soon he would forget about her completely while she would always cling on to her memories of their time together.

'Enjoying yourself, Priya?' Mac asked, coming over to her, an almost welcome interruption to her introspections.

'Yes. It's been brilliant.'

'I hear the dancers are going to invite us to join them in the centre soon. You should prepare yourself.'

'To be honest, Mac, I'm getting a bit of a headache. The incense probably. I may go back to my room and take a quick nap. I'll join you all later. It's going to be a long night.'

He nodded but didn't say anything. She was sure her absences most evenings had been noticed by her co-workers. She still tried to spend as much time with them as she could, wanting to get to know them properly in case she worked with them in the future. But she couldn't give up the brief moments of time she got to spend with Rohan.

She was also sure many people suspected she had a lover, although she doubted anyone would guess it was Rohan. She wasn't the only team member who'd found romance on the island. But as long as they were safe, and it wasn't interfering with their work, as far as Priya was concerned it was none of her business. She hoped they gave her the same courtesy.

As she started walking back to the palace grounds, her thoughts about Rohan, and the conservation project, and his wedding, and his queen came flooding back. Why it did it matter so much to her? When she'd heard a previous boyfriend of hers had married, she hadn't batted an eyelid. Their relationship was over—she'd done her crying at the time. But Rohan made her feel cherished and adored in a way she'd never experienced before. Was that the reason why it felt different this time even though she'd gone into this relationship with open eyes? She wasn't the kind of person who expected weddings and doting husbands and children to be in her future.

She'd accepted the reality of becoming involved with a prince and she knew she wasn't good enough to be his queen. There was no future for them. So why was she having so much trouble with the idea Rohan was getting married soon?

She slowed her pace as she approached the garden, taking some breaths to calm herself. She didn't want Rohan to guess at any of her turbulent thoughts. He was already far too perceptive.

Inside the garden, there were a few lanterns dotted around the wall but most of the area was in shadow. When she met Rohan there previously, it had heightened the romantic ambience. Now it felt lonely. For the first time ever she was a little scared of the garden.

'Hello,' she called out nervously.

'Hi,' a deep rumble came from the trees. Warmth flooded through her when she heard Rohan's voice. All of a sudden, her concerns and fears dissolved away, comforted by his presence.

As Rohan stepped into the light, she sighed with relief. A small part of her had worried Rohan's message was because something bad had happened. But she could see he looked all right. He looked more than all right. He looked rakishly handsome in his cream prince's jacket with gold-and-red kalka pattern on his sleeves and his rich red epaulettes with gold brocade.

He took one of her hands in each of his and gave them a light squeeze. 'Hi,' he said again with an irresistible grin.

'Hi,' she replied with a light laugh. 'What are you doing here? Shouldn't you be waltzing around a dance floor somewhere?'

'There's a refreshment break.' His fingers gently stroked her palms causing her body to heat. She made an effort to be sensible.

'Then aren't you expected to chat with your potential brides? Won't they be looking for you?' She tried hard to keep the bitterness from her tone but his questioning look showed she hadn't succeeded.

'I told my family I would be in my rooms for twenty minutes.'

'Okay.' So why was he in the garden with her instead? He didn't seem in any hurry to tell her his reason.

'How is your party?' he asked.

'It's good. Probably not as dignified as yours, but a lot of fun.'

'I wish I could go to your party instead.'

'You're the prince. I'm sure you could go anywhere you want.'

'I have much less freedom than you would imagine.'

She sighed. She couldn't argue with that. Beyond their one weekend away, Rohan didn't have the freedom to be with her the way she wanted them to be.

And she would never ask him to risk his family and his island to take a chance the tentative relationship between them could develop into something real and lasting. Not that Rohan had indicated he wanted anything more than the fling. As far as she could tell, it was only her who was thinking about love and marriage.

But it was so hard to even think about saying goodbye for good.

Rohan stood in the dusk of the garden, away from the music and crowds in the palace, enjoying the peace and Priya. She was wearing a peach lehenga choli with silver embroidery. He'd never seen her in traditional South Asian outfits before. She looked like one of the figures from his murals come to life.

He'd always found cholis flattering. But seeing Priya's, cropped below her ribs displaying her taut stomach; he wanted nothing more than to run his tongue from the edge of her blouse across her skin, past her navel and lower.

He groaned.

'Rohan, are you feeling all right.' Priya came close to him, putting her hand on his arm, concern clear on her face.

'I'm fine. How is your party?'

'Good,' she replied slowly, with a puzzled look.

Of course, he'd just asked her that. He'd spent hours politely escorting different women, selected by his parents, to the dance floor. They were all beautiful, intelligent and accomplished, but he didn't want to be with them. The only woman who could remotely hold his interest wasn't in the room.

His parents were beginning to look concerned that despite him spending the previous day sailing, games in the garden that morning and many lavish meals getting to know his female guests better, there weren't any he was inclined to invite to stay longer.

He certainly hadn't laid his eyes on any of the women and known instinctively she was the one he was going to marry the way his parents claimed they had—he'd never understood why his parents felt the need to make up a story about it. It was clear to anyone who saw them together there was deep affection between them, stronger because it grew as they got more comfortable with each other.

It was what he had wished for in his marriage. *Had* wished for? He still wished for that kind of marriage, didn't he?

'How have the events gone so far? Is everything going to plan?' Priya asked.

He frowned. She was doing that thing where she made polite small talk to cover deeper thoughts. He would indulge her for a short while, but then he was digging into what was bothering her.

'Yes, all going to plan,' he replied. 'No mishaps. Not that any would be allowed. Every eventuality and contingency has been accounted for.' Every eventuality except him not choosing his future queen.

'What are you doing tomorrow? I heard there's six or seven events going on during the day. But surely you can't be doing all of them. Or is there a secret agenda for the royal family and specially chosen guests?'

Why was she trying so hard to make conversation? They never usually had this difficulty. Normally when they were together, they talked about anything and everything— how their day had gone, about the island. The only topic they stayed away from was the future they weren't going to share. With the ball, the future was intruding where it wasn't welcome. No wonder Priya was subdued. He couldn't deny he was also feeling low. Defeated.

He sighed. He knew what he was supposed to be doing with his life. And it wasn't standing in his garden with a beautiful woman he could never marry.

Perhaps ordinary conversation would have to do. 'My family usually have a lie-in the day after the ball. I've never known the gala to end until the early hours and I'll be expected to stay until the last guest leaves or the band stops playing from sheer exhaustion. My parents will probably retire in a few hours or so though.'

She was silent, walking through the garden, softly humming to herself. 'And your guests? Have you met anyone interesting?'

He furrowed his brow. Was she asking about women? Her tone was so matter of fact, as if she didn't care he may have been talking to the woman he was going to marry.

'Plenty of interesting guests. I've been spending a lot of time with potential investors—a couple of hotel chains. They like the sound of the summer palace. I'm going to show them round before they leave.'

She tilted her head and gave him a look of amused exasperation. 'Now, Rohan. I don't think that's the kind of merger your family have in mind.'

He'd never thought of his name as particularly pretty before. But on Priya's lips, in the darkness, it sounded lyrical, sensual.

'You haven't been to the summer palace yet,' he said. 'You should come with me when I give them the tour.'

She straightened suddenly. 'Does it have murals you want me to inspect?' she asked, with a stiffness to her tone.

'No.'

'Then that's hardly going to be appropriate, is it? I'm sure there'll be other guests who would love to see it though.'

He blinked against her harsh words. 'I suppose you're right,' he replied.

'Why did you ask me to meet you here?' she asked, meeting his eyes directly.

He could hear the orchestra start to play their next set. He didn't have much longer before he had to choose his next dance partner. Although he knew exactly who that person would be if he had the freedom of true choice.

He wanted to dance with Priya in the grand ballroom. To whisk her round the room and hear her laugh from sheer exuberance. Since it wasn't an option, he would settle for the only thing he could.

'Would you honour me with this dance?' he asked, bowing as he held out her hand.

Priya stared at him, scrutinising him with her dark, round eyes, as if making a momentous decision. He held his breath. Finally she smiled, dipped into a curtsey and replied, 'I would be delighted, kind sir.'

He gathered her to him, her body fitting perfectly against his. Sparks flew where his hand rested on the bare skin above her waist. He didn't think this feeling would ever dissipate.

He led her round the garden, in an old-fashioned waltz, making the moves up since those weren't in the lessons from his tutor.

By the time the music came to an end, they were breathless and laughing. Instead of releasing her, he gathered her closer to him, letting go of her hand so he could cradle her neck. Her lips parted as he lowered his head towards her.

An alarm went off.

'My break's over,' Rohan said. 'I'll have to go back in a few minutes.'

Priya extracted herself from Rohan's arms, and walked over to the bench. His alarm was the sobering bucket of cold water she needed to bring her back to the stark reality there was a gulf between them. He was leaving her this evening, but ultimately he would walk away from her for good. There was no compromise solution for them. There was no *them*.

Rohan sat next to her. He looked worried. 'Is everything all right, Priya?'

'Well, I shouldn't keep you from your guests,' she replied, getting ready to stand. Rohan placed a restraining hand on her arm.

'What's wrong, Priya?'

'Nothing's wrong. You need to go back.'

'I wish I didn't have to. I wish I could stay here with you all night.'

Her body was a mass of contradictions, buzzing with exhilaration at the certain knowledge of how much he wanted her while at the same time heavy with despair because it didn't matter what they both wished. He couldn't stay with her.

'But you have to return. You have no choice,' she said.

'And it annoys you?'

'Annoys me?' Her voice rose an octave. 'No. It doesn't annoy me. You have a duty to perform. We both know that.' Suddenly her confused emotions bubbled to the surface. 'But what are we doing here tonight, Rohan? What have we been doing for the past couple of weeks? It's madness. You said yourself you aren't in a position to offer me a relationship. And I know you're expected to find your wife from these events. What do you want from me?'

Rohan opened his mouth but nothing came out.

Priya stood, steeling herself for what she needed to say. 'We should have gone back to the way things were when we came back from our weekend. Our affair was a moment out of time and it's all it should have been. It was a mistake trying to prolong it. I was living in a fantasy and now it's over.' She tried to keep the bitterness from her voice as she said, 'This isn't a fairy tale. Not for me. It's time for you to go back to being Rohan Varma, Yuvaraja, and I'll go back to being…me.'

'I see,' he said in a clipped tone.

She waited, hoping, daring to believe he could tell her she was wrong and there was a way they could get a happily ever after. He didn't.

'I'd better go.' She took a few steps, then turned back and kissed him on the cheek. 'Goodbye, Rohan. I hope you meet someone who'll make you a wonderful wife. You deserve all the happiness in the world.'

CHAPTER FIFTEEN

A WEEK LATER, the gala was over, the decorations were being taken down, the palace was being returned to its usual state and Priya was back at work on preserving the murals.

Although it was unlikely she would bump into Rohan accidentally, she was on tenterhooks. The last time she'd seen him was when they danced in his garden.

It had felt like she was caught in a whirlwind, transported into a magical place—Cinderella at the ball. It almost came as a shock to find the fireworks she'd seen as they waltzed round the garden were only figments of her imagination.

Walking away from him after his alarm went off, actually she ran away, was the hardest thing she'd ever done. She still didn't know where her resolve had come from. She'd gone straight to her room and let the tears fall freely.

She cried for the young teenager who grew up unwanted and unloved. And she cried for the young woman who had started to open her heart to a man who left her in no doubt that she was very much wanted, desired and cared for. But someone she could never have.

Since that night, even though she told herself she didn't expect to hear from him, she was still disappointed when she hadn't received any messages.

Seven days. It was the longest they'd ever gone without seeing each other since their first meeting on the balcony.

She'd held on to this false hope that, despite her parting words, he'd ask to meet her again in the garden. And despite any words of common sense telling her it was futile and would bring nothing but heartache, she knew she would run to him.

But she heard nothing.

The palace was still abuzz with speculation on whether any of the guests who were staying on had captured Rohan's interest. Had he found someone he could see himself spending the rest of his life with? Was that why he hadn't got in touch. Did she really want to know? Why was she torturing herself?

Priya took a deep breath and stepped back from the mural she was working on. The paintwork was too delicate for her to continue unless she could give the task her full concentration. She cleared away her tools and told her team she was taking a quick break to get some fresh air; it wasn't unusual for her team to do that since they were working with harsh chemicals.

Once outside she wandered into the woods, purposely walking away from the direction of Rohan's garden.

What was going on with her?

This wasn't the first time one of her relationships had ended. In the past, work had been her solace. She had always been able to distract herself from anything in her life by concentrating on the detailed preservations she was doing. Why was she finding it so hard this time?

The answer was simple. This was the first time her heart was truly broken.

She'd heard broken hearts can heal over time. She'd assumed it was true because she'd got over her previous boyfriends. But what she felt for them hadn't been a fraction of the strength and depth of her feelings for Rohan.

She loved him.

The realisation didn't come as a shock once she'd admitted it. It had been creeping on her for weeks, surfacing on the night of the ball but remaining unacknowledged, unnamed.

It wasn't only a physical attraction but an attraction of minds and souls.

She could try telling herself she was being fanciful, or she was confusing lust and love, as she had before. But it would be doing a disservice to her heart.

How could she not love someone as wonderful as Rohan? He made her feel loved, valued and protected every moment they spent together. He showed her in his countless thoughtful gestures that he cared about her. Of course she loved him.

This wasn't a flame that would shine brightly then burn out, but a banyan tree that would only grow and strengthen with time.

As if on autopilot her feet were taking her back towards the path which led to Rohan's garden. She stopped and turned round. From now on, Rohan would go there with his family, which would one day soon include his wife and later on his children. It was closed to her.

But her heart didn't want to listen. She loved Rohan. She wanted to run and find him so she could tell him how she felt. Beg for more time with him.

To what end though? He could never be with her. He hadn't contacted her in seven days—he was already staying away from her. He had a duty to his family and to the island. What made her think she was worth him turning his back on it?

Nothing.

She had nothing to offer. She'd been ignored and forgotten by her father. Dumped by a boyfriend for 'someone better' on more than one occasion. She was nobody. A nothing.

She had no right to think Rohan could abandon his duty or he would refuse to do what was expected of him just because she loved him and wanted to be with him.

He wasn't meant for her. It didn't matter how she felt. They weren't destined to be together.

And if she stayed on Adysara working on the sites she'd visited with Rohan, she would never get the chance to heal. Her heart would break even more as he forgot about her and moved on with his life.

She gave a bitter laugh. Here she was with the possibility of the chance of a lifetime to work on a culturally significant project and she didn't think she could do it.

It should have been a dream. Instead it was a nightmare.

For the first time since she had heard about the caves, she wished she'd never seen them.

She headed back to the palace where Mac

was waiting to tell her Mr Agrawal wanted to see her.

As soon as she approached Mr Agrawal's office she noticed Rohan's assistant waiting outside. She licked her lips unsure whether she was hoping Rohan wanted to see her or hoping he didn't so she wouldn't have to face him again so soon after her revelation.

The assistant escorted her to Rohan's study.

He was standing next to the window when she entered. The afternoon light should have been harsh, casting shadows across his nose and jaw. Instead it emphasised the perfection of his features.

She loved him. She could never be with him. She would laugh if it wasn't so poignant.

'Priya.' He smiled at her, gesturing for her to take a seat on the couch. 'Thank you for coming.'

He was polite but distant. That was good. That's what she needed. She noticed he looked at the door and give a small signal to his assistant who handed him a folder then left. She hadn't realised they weren't alone.

After sitting opposite her, Rohan stared at her, a strange smile playing on his face. He was so gorgeous. She wanted to reach across the gap and fling herself onto his lap.

She shifted in her seat. This wasn't going

to help her situation. She had to go into protective mode.

'How have you been?' he asked.

'Good thanks,' she answered, deliberately
using a tone of polite distance.

'I missed you.'

She stiffened. His words didn't help her
resolve. 'You wanted to see me?'

He beamed. 'I have some wonderful news
for you. About the island.'

'What is it?'

'The hotel companies I met with are interested in investing. With the money we can get
from leasing the summer palace, my family
can finance the preservation of the caves ourselves. We won't need government backing.'

'Wonderful.' His face was the happiest
she'd ever seen it and she couldn't help re-
sponding to his unbridled joy. She wanted to
hug him. Luckily, being seated would have
made it awkward. 'What does it mean, your
family's financing it?'

'Because we don't have to go through the
government's policy approval and procure-
ment process, we can start the work immediately and sign the contract with your company.
I spoke to Toby MacFarlane and Govinda
Agrawal already. They're ready to proceed.

And we'd like you to lead.' He paused giving her an expectant smile.

This was it. The moment her dreams should have come true. Turning this down was one of the hardest things she would do. But it would be harder if she stayed on Adysara and had to watch while Rohan got engaged then married. She had to walk away from him, leave him before she was forced to watch him leave her for good.

'No!' she called out.

'What?' Rohan visibly started at her unexpected response.

'I don't want it this way.'

'What do you mean?'

She didn't want Rohan to know she loved him. It wouldn't help anyone. She tried to come up with a valid reason for her refusal. 'If I get the role I want to know... I need to know I got it on my own merits.' That sounded feasible. It also had the benefit of being true—she would want to know that.

'But you have got it on your merits. I've seen how skilled and proficient you are. You have the qualifications.'

'I know I'm qualified. But our relationship will always make me question whether it was a factor.'

'I can assure you I would not let my emotional attachment affect important decisions,' he replied, his posture and tone stiff. Her heart leapt at his causal reference to his feelings. But now she'd offended him.

'Rohan, I really appreciate your trust in my abilities. It means the world to me. But I can't stay on Adysara. I'll help Mac recruit someone suitable, but as soon as Leo Blake is able to come over, I'm returning to England.' She held her breath.

'No,' he replied. 'You can't do that. I won't allow it.'

'Please, Rohan. Can't you understand how hard this is going to be for me?'

'No. This work is too important to me. If you're worried about favouritism or nepotism or anything like that, I can assure you I didn't make this decision alone. You are the most qualified person to lead this work. If you don't accept then I'll need to scope different companies.'

Priya bent her head. She couldn't tell Rohan the real reason she wanted to leave. And she couldn't let her co-workers miss out on the opportunity to work on this massive conservation project just because she'd had the monumental stupidity to fall in love with a prince.

What she wanted was of no importance. She had no choice but to accept.

* * *

After Priya left, Rohan went out onto his balcony staring over the gardens. It had taken months to get the palace and grounds ready for the gala festivities and only days to dismantle it.

But time was surprising. It was really only two months since he'd met Priya, but he felt she knew him better than anyone, even his own family. And he'd thought he knew her too.

He was still reeling from her admission she didn't want to take the lead on their project. And in his mind it had always been *their* project. She was the first person who could envisage the same possibilities he did, who shared his values on accessible art versus protection. He'd expected her to hug him from happiness. Instead she'd turned him down.

Not only that, she didn't want to work on the project at all. She wanted to return to England.

It had been her dream to work on the conservation of stone-cut sculptures. She'd admitted it to him.

He was right to refuse to accept her decision. She was being irrational, worried their relationship had clouded his judgement. As if he would let his feelings affect something so important to the prosperity of the island.

He'd already discussed the situation with Agrawal and Mac before mentioning the proposal to Priya. In fact it was Mac who suggested Priya with Agrawal supporting the suggestion. They had assured him his initial assessment of her abilities was correct and she was the perfect person to lead the project.

A buzz from his intercom brought Rohan back through to his study. His assistant entered to tell him one of the hoteliers who'd discussed potential investment was still on the island and wanted to meet him.

Rohan needed a distraction from thinking about Priya so he arranged to meet with the hotelier immediately.

After his meeting he went to his parents' rooms. There wouldn't be any government business for his father since they still had guests.

Rohan closed his eyes. Those guests were out during the day on excursions, but he would be expected to have dinner with them and entertain them over drinks afterwards. He inwardly cursed the tradition which prolonged the gala by inviting select people to continue their visit. It happened after every gala, but this year everyone knew the reasons behind the invitations.

'Rohan, I wasn't expecting to see you so

early,' his mother greeted him. 'But I'm glad you came. I wanted to talk about our guests with you, since you didn't ask me to invite anyone specific.'

'Of course, Mother,' he said, taking a seat opposite her and his father. She looked frustrated with him. He grimaced. He hated that he'd upset her.

His parents had been, understandably, disappointed when he hadn't found any of the charming women who'd attended the gala charming enough to ask for an extended stay. Instead, he'd spent most of the gala chatting with the hotel magnates. His mother had to take matters into her own hands and had invited the families she thought would be most suitable.

How he hated the word *suitable*. What did it actually mean? An impeccable blood line. More wealth than more people could imagine. It didn't make a difference; it was his duty to meet these women and select one to marry.

He ran a finger around his collar, as if by doing so he could loosen the burden of his duty.

'But before we talk about our guests, I want to update you on further discussions I've had with one of the hoteliers,' Rohan said. 'They've updated their proposal.'

'This is the man who's prepared to increase his investment contingent on the tourist flow we can expect if the wall painting and caves are attractions?' his father asked.

'That's right. He thinks there's potential for making the summer palace and its surrounding area an island paradise. But if we can offer the historical artwork too, maybe gain World Heritage status…well you know what it would mean for our country's finances. And he's prepared to part finance the work as a grant.'

'A grant?' his father perked up at hearing his family wouldn't have to invest as much upfront.

'That's right. This is a great company. Very focused on eco-tourism. Whether or not they offer the best financial package, I would be inclined to go with them. And we'd be able to start almost immediately.'

'And the project team's ready?'

'Yes. On standby.' Rohan pressed his lips together as he recalled his conversation with Priya. 'I have to admit there was some uncertainty around the person I've chosen as lead. She was thinking about returning to England, but I've persuaded her to stay, I think.' He hoped.

'This woman,' his father said, 'Priya Sen

isn't it? I hear you've been spending a lot of time with her.'

'Yes, she was doing the scoping investigation.'

'And you went with her to Aurangabad.'

'That's right. We wanted to examine Ajanta and Ellora for ideas on presenting the caves.'

'What's her background? Where are her family from?'

'I don't know all the details,' he lied. 'She doesn't come from royalty or wealth, if that's what you're interested in.' He noticed the look which passed between his parents. He shouldn't have spoken to them so sharply. 'You have no need to worry,' he told them. 'She only considers me a client. She's leading on the preservation work. That's all. I know my duty.'

'But...' his mother began.

'Please excuse me, I still have a lot to do. I'm going to return to my rooms. I'll see you at dinner.'

Once back in his study, Rohan sat at his desk and pulled up a paper about his regeneration proposal.

He should be happy. Everything was falling into place. His family were finally on board with his plans to increase tourism. Buildings which had remained empty would soon be useful again. And, slowly but surely the wall painting and the caves would be preserved then restored.

The project would take years. He knew the team members would change over time, and in the long term they hoped to bring in conservators from India or other neighbouring countries to share and develop expertise. But at least Priya would be with them for a few years. He would still get to see her and spend time with her.

He froze. No, he couldn't. He would be married. It was his duty.

The thought of her being on the island, of having meetings with her for status reports, but not being able to hold her again, or meet with her alone again, was unbearable. And once he was married, he couldn't spend any time with Priya. It would be wrong. It would be unfair to both her and his wife.

No wonder she said she couldn't stay on the island. He would want to get away too. He grimaced as he recalled his implicit threat he would consider putting out for tender if she didn't lead it.

She'd said it was too hard to stay. What if her initial refusal wasn't about favouritism, but because she couldn't bear the idea of working in proximity to him when he was married to someone else.

He ran his finger around his collar again. This was an impossible situation.

If Priya took on the role, then he would hand the project to his assistant to oversee or make it part of Summer Palace Island's regeneration project so it wasn't under the royal family any longer. If his father kept to his plan of abdicating in five years, the long length of the project meant Rohan wouldn't be able to have direct oversight anyway, since he would be king.

Stepping away from the project was the best option for all of them, even if Priya still wanted to return to England. He hoped she would lead the work—she really was the best person for the job. But he couldn't bear the idea of her being unhappy so he would also let her know she could return to England if she still wanted.

He couldn't risk meeting her, not when he knew one smile from her and he would blurt out how much he wanted to be with her. He took the coward's way out and sent her a text message.

CHAPTER SIXTEEN

PRIYA READ THE message for the fifth time. Rohan wrote that he would be stepping away from the project, but he'd changed his mind and she could return to England instead if she still preferred to leave. Very short, very succinct.

She understood the subtext—he was letting her go.

Not wanting to be alone with her thoughts, Priya left her room and forced herself to join the rest of her team in the recreation room. Fortunately, they were watching a film so she was able to zone out without anyone noticing.

Why had he let her go? Only hours before, he'd categorically refused to accept her decision to return to England. What had changed in that short time?

She should be happy. Ecstatic. Hadn't she got what she wanted?

For the first time in her life, someone had

put her wishes above their own. Prioritised what she wanted.

She'd never felt more miserable.

Not wanting to waste time, Priya went to speak to Mac to let him know her decision. He looked stunned.

'Priya, are you sure about this?' he asked. 'I mean, you can take annual leave once the palace mural is finished. But I thought you'd be eager to work on the stone murals and sculptures. It's exactly in your sphere of expertise. I hoped to have my best person on the job.'

'Your best person?' Priya couldn't help repeating. Had he really said that about her?

'Yes. I had hoped you'd be part of the initial palace project. You sounded keen when I talked to you about it, but you didn't submit an expression of interest for the lead role.'

'Leo said he wanted to do it. I know he has more experience than me. I was hoping you'd select me to be part of the team though,' she admitted.

'Priya, let me be frank. When you didn't apply for the team lead position, I assumed you didn't want to work abroad for an extended period. Sorry for assuming, but I specifically spoke to you about applying and you chose not to. If you'd put yourself forward, the position would have been yours.'

Priya sat in shocked silence, absorbing what she'd been told. She had been devastated when she wasn't selected for the team. She had no idea he'd taken her failure to express her interest as a sign she didn't want to work abroad.

'Priya, you can be honest with me. Is your indecision because of your relationship with Yuvaraja?'

Priya had thought nothing could surprise her more than hearing she was first choice for the project. She was wrong. The expression on Mac's face was concern rather than anger.

'Perhaps I should have told you about it,' Priya began.

'Why? It wasn't any of my business. You weren't breaking any ethical or company guidelines. The only reason it was brought up was because Yuvaraja wanted to make sure we were aware he had a conflict of interest when Agrawal and I proposed you lead the work.'

'Rohan told you?'

'It was appropriate for him to do so.'

'Of course. I didn't think.'

'I don't understand all the ins and outs of your relationship. And I have no reason to. But don't let a love affair that ran its course affect the trajectory of what could be an amazing career. I see huge things in your future, Priya. Think about it.'

After Priya left Mac she went for a walk. Despite being distracted, she stopped to speak briefly to people as she passed them. As well as her co-workers, she'd got to know the palace staff who lived in the buildings near hers. If she stayed on Adysara and worked on the project she would get to know more people and her sense of belonging would grow. She still couldn't believe she could have been working here months ago if only she'd put herself forward.

How many times had she let an opportunity pass her by because she didn't think she was good enough, or worth it? Because of her own low expectations?

When had she learnt to expect nothing but rejection and disappointment? It was an easy question to answer. After her father left her at boarding school, always putting work and travel above her, she'd got used to never being a priority. But she hadn't recognised just how far she'd let her father's abandonment cloud her perception of herself.

A part of her still longed for some kind of relationship with her father and stepmother, but if that never happened she would be all right. Just because her dad didn't care about her didn't mean she was worthless.

But if she wanted others to see that, she needed to believe it herself first.

It was okay for her to stand up for what she wanted. Sometimes she would put herself forward and she would get knocked back. It was fine. It would be a disappointment, but she was strong enough to get back on her feet.

So what did she want now? She sighed. She wanted Rohan.

But it was one thing to put herself forward for a job. She couldn't apply the same philosophy to her love life and beg Rohan to be with her. Could she?

Priya rolled her eyes. Of course she couldn't. Rohan was Yuvaraja of Adysara. He had always been honest with her that he couldn't marry her—had admitted to her he needed to make a match which would bring some material advantage to his country. She certainly had nothing to offer in that regard.

Besides, he'd told her he didn't think people really fell in love. He believed true love was a 'hormonal myth'. He probably didn't care about her the same way.

Why invite that kind of rejection?

Priya stopped where she was. It was exactly the kind of thinking she'd been scolding herself for.

What would she have to lose in reality if she told Rohan how she felt? What was the worst that could happen? He could turn her down. She fully expected him to. He'd already told her he wasn't free to choose who he married. She'd told him she accepted it. And she did.

But since their first kiss next to the megalith, they'd agreed nothing more could happen between them and each time they kept going back to each other. It had to mean something.

Was she being naive thinking Rohan could have feelings for her? Could he feel more than sexual attraction? He'd never said anything about the way he felt.

But then she'd never told him she loved him either.

She'd never expected to fall in love. She hadn't asked for it. Rohan was probably the worst person she could have chosen. But love didn't give her a choice.

She loved Rohan and she wanted a real relationship with him. She wanted them to try.

And she was worth it. She was worth putting herself out there. She was strong enough to cope if things didn't work out the way she wanted.

Taking a deep breath, she sent Rohan a text asking if he would meet her in his garden. It felt like for ever but was probably no more than a few seconds before his reply came telling her he'd be there in ten minutes.

As she made her way to the garden, Priya cursed inwardly for not giving herself time to think through what she wanted to say.

The garden door was locked. Of course it would be. It was Rohan's private garden. Nobody could enter without his permission. And she was nobody. What had she been thinking, summoning him to meet her as if she was the member of royalty, not him?

This was a terrible idea. She turned to go but had only taken a few steps when her resolve returned. She had one chance to say her piece. She wasn't going to back out now. She went to stand against the door, as if it could provide some additional backbone for her.

The minutes passed by in a flash and at the same time seemed to go on for ever before Rohan was walking towards her.

'Priya.' His smile when he noticed her made her heart soar. Hope blossomed that everything could work out the way she wanted. 'Is everything okay?'

She nodded, too overcome with emotion to

risk speaking. Rohan unlocked the door, then waited for her to precede him.

She took a couple of steps inside then, without looking at him, she said, 'I love you, Rohan.'

'What?' She couldn't interpret his tone so she slowly walked towards him trying to read his expression. But it was blank.

'I said I love you. I know we barely know each other, and I know you don't think people fall in love quickly, but I feel like you're the person who knows me best in the world.'

'Why are you telling me this?'

She didn't know what kind of response she was expecting, only what she'd been hoping for. And that definitely wasn't it.

'I wanted to tell you the truth. I love you and I want us to be together.' She spoke in a rush, relieved to finally get the words out.

'I have a duty,' he said, helplessly.

'I know. I know you have a duty to your country and your family. But I think I could be your wife. I think I could be your queen.' She gave a bitter laugh, then held up her hand when he opened his mouth. 'But I know it's impossible. I'm not asking for that. I'm not asking for marriage. I'm not expecting for ever. I don't know what the future holds. All I know for certain is I love you. I am worthy of you. I'm asking you to have a real, honest, not secret relationship with me, for as long as it may last.'

'Priya.' He swallowed.

She formed her hands into fists, drumming up every ounce of courage she had left. 'I'm here, Rohan, doing the scariest thing I've ever done in my life. I'm telling you how I feel. I'm telling you what I want. Because I love you. All I'm asking for is more time for us. With no expectations. I know you're supposed to be choosing your future bride now, but I'm asking for you, right now, to choose me instead. For as long as you can. Put me first. Choose me.'

Priya held her breath and hoped. And she hoped. Then she bent her head with dejection as she learnt how fragile hope could be.

CHAPTER SEVENTEEN

CHOOSE ME.

Priya's words repeated themselves in Rohan's head as he sat at his desk the following morning trying to absorb the figures on the spreadsheet in front of him.

Choose me.

She'd waited for him to respond, her expression nervous but hopeful. And he'd done nothing. Just stared at her. After a few minutes Priya had nodded her head, as if his silence was the answer she had expected, smiled sweetly and then left.

Even after she'd gone, he'd stood there like an idiot until his assistant messaged that he was expected for dinner. As he'd left the garden, he'd started in the direction of her quarters, tempted to go after her.

Like he wanted to go to look for her now. But what would be the point? There was nothing he could say that could change their situation. He wasn't free to choose her.

Rohan gave up on deciphering the report and went to stand out on his balcony. Usually standing there helped him relax and calm his thoughts. But not today.

Choose me.

What response had Priya expected him to give her? Did she want him to disappoint his parents, his people, his country for a few more months with her?

How dare she put him in this position? He was Yuvaraja of Adysara. He prided himself on always being open at the beginning of any relationship, letting girlfriends know from the outset he couldn't offer them anything long-term. He never lied to anyone about it. He'd been upfront and honest with Priya that he had a duty to make an advantageous marriage. He loved his country, but his country needed proper investment and economic growth. Without it Adysara would decline and even lose its independence. He couldn't allow that to happen. He didn't have the freedom she did to choose who she married, or, with the expectation now on him to find a bride soon, even who he had a relationship with.

Just as quickly as it had risen, his anger left him. It wasn't a fair reaction. He'd let his frustration at the situation cloud his thinking.

All Priya had done was stand up for what she wanted. Put everything on the line to do that. He knew what it would have taken for her. He grinned, wishing he could tell her how proud he was—how he wanted to applaud her.

She was so brave telling him how she felt. Telling him she loved him. His heart had beaten so fast he thought it would explode from his chest when he heard her say those words.

Three little words. He never expected such a simple phrase could have so much power over him.

But love wasn't enough. People fell in and out of love so quickly—and he'd seen, in close friends, the hurt caused when a love affair ended. He'd always been grateful it was an emotion he hadn't experienced before. He'd also seen how love and affection could come after marriage and be strong and lasting— he was a product of that kind of love—he'd convinced himself that kind of love was better because it came from companionship and shared values. Because of that belief, Rohan had never objected to carrying out his duty before. He thought by making his family and his people happy, he would be happy too.

The way he was feeling now wasn't remotely close to happy. Rohan released a slow, miserable sigh.

How could he feel happy when his lack of response, his inaction, had made Priya unhappy? She'd become so important to him his happiness depended on hers.

The previous evening, Priya hadn't told him whether she'd decided to take on the role or not. Or perhaps she had, he didn't remember much other than her saying she loved him and asking him to choose her.

He hoped she would take the role—he knew it would make her happy. Theoretically he would be happy too, simply knowing she was. But whether Priya took the role or not, he couldn't see her any more. And how could he be truly happy when he was letting the love of his life walk out of it.

Rohan clasped onto the balcony railings. The love of his life. Priya was the love of his life.

How was it, he was only able to admit to himself the true depth of his feelings now, when it was too late. But now he had admitted it he couldn't help repeating it—he loved her. He wanted to rush to her side, to gather her in his arms and to feel her heart beat in time with his as he told her how much he loved her.

If she really loved him too, if the way she

felt was one scintilla of how much he adored her then perhaps they could—

No, he didn't want to think about it. Couldn't let himself wish for that possibility. It would make things so much harder. He wasn't free to act on his feelings. He needed to bury them deep if he had any hope of doing his duty to make an advantageous marriage.

He laughed without humour. This suitable wife he was supposed to marry seemed more hypothetical every second. How could he promise forever to another woman when the only woman that pervaded his thoughts, who filled his heart and soul with joy, was Priya— someone who wasn't meant to be his.

Rohan wanted to yell. To rail against his fate. He accepted he lived a privileged life. He knew it came with responsibility. With duty. He had never shirked his duty.

But he'd never been in love before.

How could he ever contemplate marrying someone else when his heart belonged to Priya? How could he do his duty to his people and his country if he couldn't be true to himself?

Priya had asked him to choose her. What were his choices? He could do what was expected of him, marry someone of his parents' choosing. It wouldn't matter who. He could never love that woman, but he knew there were women who would accept a loveless marriage for the privilege of being queen.

Or he could follow his heart and risk everything for Priya.

The thought scared him. How he felt for Priya scared him. The feelings were new. They made him vulnerable. What if those feelings left as quickly as they came? Not for him. But he was worried Priya's feelings would fade or she'd realise she made a mistake.

What would happen if he gave up everything for her and she stopped loving him?

Not that she'd asked him to give up anything. She hadn't asked for ever. She'd only asked for a longer relationship. Perhaps it's all she wanted.

He discarded that notion. No, Priya had said she knew it was impossible for her to be his queen. She'd asked for what she thought she could get.

All Priya had asked was for him to delay choosing a potential bride until their relationship had run its course.

It was a foolish suggestion. If he and Priya started a real, out in the open relationship, the way he felt wasn't going to 'run its course'. His love was the never-ending, undying kind. And Priya wasn't the sort of woman who did things by half measures either. When she gave her heart for real, she would give it whole-heartedly.

He wanted to spend the rest of his life with Priya. He couldn't imagine any other woman being his wife. If Priya decided to return to England, he would go with her. Priya was his world. He had to be with her.

His choice was simple.

With the weight of making his decision removed, Rohan could breathe easily again. There was still a lot to do. He had to make plans for seeing Priya and telling her how he felt.

But first, he needed to speak to his parents. He went to their rooms. If they were surprised to see him so early in the day they didn't say anything. His mother's welcoming smile gave him the courage to begin.

'Father, Mother, I love you.' He swallowed when he saw the concerned expression on his parents' faces at his declaration. His parents had always supported him and encouraged him to strive to make his dreams come true. He never wanted to disappoint them, but he had to make them understand how he felt. He took a deep breath. 'I respect you as my parents and as my Maharaja and Maharani. I love the people of Adysara and my country. You know I have always tried to live up to your expectations. I've always done my duty when I could. Now I need to tell you something.'

'Of course, beta,' his father replied.

'You can tell us anything, darling,' his mother agreed.

'I've chosen the woman I want as my wife and yuvarani.'

'Well, that's wonderful news,' his mother said. 'You had me worried for a moment.'

He noticed his father reach out and cover his mother's hand, clearly sensing there was more to come. 'Carry on, Rohan,' he said. 'She's not one of our guests, is she?'

Rohan shook his head. 'No. It's Priya. Priya Sen.'

His mother furrowed her brow. 'Isn't that the art conservator?'

'Yes. She's amazingly talented at her work. You should hear her proposals for the caves. She's incredible.'

His parents exchanged glances.

'Beta, if you aren't ready to get married yet, if you need more time, then there's no hurry. You don't have to choose someone straightaway,' his father said. 'Spend some time with this Priya if you want to.'

Rohan straightened. Did his parents think he was indulging in a brief fling or having a small rebellion against his duty? He was all too aware of what his decision to marry Priya would mean for Adysara.

'I love Priya,' he said, with a quiet determination. 'I don't need more time. I love her. I want to marry her.'

His parents were silent. Looking at each other and him with concerned expressions.

He hated that he was worrying them; that he was disappointing them. He had to make them understand how difficult this was for him, but also how important Priya was to his happiness.

'Adysara means so much to me,' he said, 'I will do anything to improve life on the island for our people and help us remain independent. I know that would have been easier and faster if I married someone who could help with our country's growth. But I'm certain Adysara will prosper anyway—we have the basic infrastructure and we can find other ways to bring in investment. Maybe if I hadn't met Priya I would have married one of the lovely women you've introduced me to and I probably would have been happy. But I have met Priya and I can't be with anyone else now. I love her.'

He noticed the sheen of tears in his mother's

eyes. He would always regret that his choice made her sad but he couldn't lose Priya.

His mother reached out her hand. 'We love you, beta. All we want is for you to be happy. Come,' she said.

'Yes, Rohan, come over here,' his father added, 'Tell us all about this wonderful woman. Our future daughter-in-law and yuvarani. When can we meet her?'

Rohan went over to embrace both his parents.

'I'll contact the wedding planner,' his mother said as they all broke apart. 'We have so much to organise.'

Rohan laughed. He shouldn't have doubted their love for him would support his decision. They would learn to love Priya too. But not nearly as much as he loved her.

CHAPTER EIGHTEEN

PRIYA STOOD IN front of the mural her team had been working on since the gala ended. It had been in better condition than the other ones they'd completed and would probably only take a few more days to finish.

'Mac wants to speak to you, Priya,' one of her team members said after returning from her break.

'Did he say it was urgent?' she asked.

'He said whenever you're free. But you know Mac. He probably means now.'

Priya grinned as she removed her gloves. Since she didn't know how long she'd be away, Priya left instructions for the other members to adjust for her absence, reminding them to take their breaks as necessary.

She still hadn't given Mac her decision on whether she wanted to leave Adysara. Perhaps that's why he asked to see her. She didn't have an answer for him. Working on the palace murals weren't a problem. They didn't have any association with Rohan for her.

But would Rohan's invisible presence be with her at the external murals and in the caves they visited together? Priya pursed her lips. Her work was all she had left. Rohan had promised her he would hand over the project so she wouldn't have to deal with him any more. She knew what a big gesture it was for him to make, the preservation work was vital for his regeneration plans. He was making it as easy as he could for her to stay. She would be foolish to turn down the job of a lifetime simply because she'd been a bigger fool and fallen in love with someone so far out of her reach.

And when Rohan got married? Well, then she would take a very long vacation back in England.

She was ready to give Mac her decision.

'Ah, Priya,' Mac began when she found him, 'Mr Agrawal says he's heard there's been a development at cave six. Would you mind going to take a look?'

'Of course. What kind of development?'

Mac shook his head. 'No idea. Mr Agrawal didn't know much.'

'Okay. I'll head over first thing tomorrow.'

'A car's already been arranged for you today. It's probably already outside waiting.'

Priya furrowed her brow. If the development required her urgent attention it could be something serious had happened. Cave six was the one with the palace megalith. Her stomach churned at the idea it could have been damaged.

'Go now,' Mac said, ushering her towards the exit. 'I'll make sure your team's sorted.'

There was a strange twinkle in Mac's eye and she was sure he was trying to hide a smile. But it made no sense. Perhaps, because it was such a rare sight, she'd misinterpreted his humour.

Unfortunately, as soon as she was in the car, memories she'd rather not relive flooded her mind.

It had been two days since she'd laid her heart and soul bare before Rohan. Two days. His silence, as the saying went, was deafening.

She'd allowed herself one evening to brood at the final sign her love for Rohan was going nowhere, then she'd thrown herself into her work, spending long hours on the palace murals until the light prevented her from making progress then, after work, she made sure she stayed in the common areas, never on her own.

She'd told Rohan she loved him. And he hadn't replied. He barely said three words their entire exchange.

It was surprising she hadn't cried. Yet. Perhaps she was too numb, too hollow, and the emotions hadn't had a chance to rise to the surface.

She couldn't regret the time she did have with Rohan. After her previous failed relationships, she was convinced she was done with romance. Instead, she'd been given a couple of wonderful weeks with an interesting, intelligent, thoughtful, not to mention unbelievably gorgeous man. And she would concentrate on those memories, rather than the ones that came recently.

Why should there be tears? She'd started her relationship with Rohan with her eyes open, knowing there wasn't a future. She hadn't asked for anything but the few days they would have together—a weekend away and stolen kisses in the moonlight. She had no expectations. She'd certainly hadn't expected to fall in love.

And she didn't regret asking him for longer. She was proud she'd been honest about her feelings and asked for what she wanted. She was never again going to measure her self-worth on the acceptance or rejection by other people. Not even Rohan.

Her body clenched as the car slowed down near the cave entrance. She couldn't see any signs of damage from the outside.

Was her trepidation due to the possibility her megalith was damaged or was it because she was going to be entering cave six—the cave where she kissed Rohan for the first time? This would be the perfect test for her to find out whether the ghost of his presence would make working on the caves difficult.

She first examined the rock-cut structures inside the cave but couldn't see anything had changed from her last visit. She took measurements of the humidity and light but the readings were also within safe limits. That left the megalith.

She started walking down the passageway. It was so dark, Rohan probably hadn't needed to cover her eyes. She laughed at the memory although she felt a pang in her chest.

Once in front of the megalith she stood frozen in awe, as if seeing it for the first time. At least nothing was wrong with the stone sculpture. She slowly began to walk around the structure to check for changes, taking the opportunity to examine the cliff face in case there were any visibly loose rocks.

As she was finishing her examination of the final side, she heard movement coming from the tunnel. She peeked her head round the side expecting to see her driver.

Instead, her heart began to beat at a rapid pace, her breath became shallow as if the oxygen had been sucked out from round her and her mouth went dry. Her typical reaction every time she saw Rohan.

He looked at her, as if he was drinking her in; as if it had been years rather than days since he'd seen her. The same way she was looking at him.

She was too frightened to move in case the action jolted her out of this hallucination she must be having. What was he doing here?

'Rohan,' she said, when she finally managed to find her voice. 'I didn't know you were coming. Did Mr Agrawal tell you there's been a development here too?' She gestured at the megalith. 'I can't find anything wrong. I don't think there's a problem.'

Rohan had been looking so serious, nervous almost, but when she mentioned Mr Agrawal his face broke into a wide grin.

Her heart jolted. Priya couldn't help feeling

there was something more behind his smile than relief at hearing there were no problems with the megalith, which was confirmed when Rohan said, 'I know.'

'What do you mean, you know.'

'There's nothing wrong here. I asked Agrawal to get you to come here.'

She furrowed her brow. 'I don't understand.'

'I wanted to speak to you.'

'Why here? I could have come to your study.'

Rohan's cheeks turned rosy. He looked at the ground then swallowed before saying, 'I never gave you a response the other day.'

Priya shook her head. 'It's all right. I should never have asked you. You were always honest with me about your situation. I should never have tried to ask you for more than you could give. I'm sorry I put you in that position.'

He didn't reply immediately. Instead he walked over to the front of the megalith next to one of the stone tigers guarding the palace.

'I was standing here when you hurled yourself at me to save me from the debris.'

As if she could forget.

'That was the start of everything,' he continued. The intensity of his gaze made Priya's mouth go dry. She started to shake—something she didn't understand was happening, but it was something big.

'I bet you sometimes wish I hadn't,' she said trying to diffuse the tension. 'Then we wouldn't be in this situation.'

'I think we would have ended up exactly where we are, somehow. It was fate.'

Priya couldn't suppress a slight anger towards a fate that let her fall in love with a man she could never be with.

'And I don't ever wish that moment didn't happen,' he continued. 'It was the moment I began falling in love with you.'

Hundreds of conflicting moods and emotions rushed through her. He loved her. She was ecstatic. He loved her and she loved him and it was the greatest gift.

He was still the crown prince. It didn't change anything in the long run. Despair overpowered her. Why did he have to tell her he loved her? It made everything worse.

Unless he was trying to say he was prepared to have a real relationship with her. That he was delaying his duty to find a bride for a few more months with her.

'You're choosing me?' she said, holding her breath as she waited for his response.

'Yes,' he replied with the cheeky smile she loved so much.

Letting out a yelp of joy she ran into his arms. He picked her up and twirled her around. Both of them laughing from giddy happiness. Lowering her back to the ground, he ran his fingers through her hair, moving to her nape and drawing her closer for a kiss.

'We should get back to the palace,' Rohan suggested.

Priya nodded. Their passion, as always, threatened to overwhelm them. She wanted to get somewhere private. Where they could talk. There was still a lot for them to discuss. Eager as she was to make love with Rohan soon, it was sensible to make sure everything was out in the open.

He'd chosen her. She couldn't believe it was real.

The journey back to the palace was torture. Rohan had sent her driver away so they both went in his limo. They had the privacy screen up but after a few minutes on Rohan's lap, the bumpy road dictated safety came first and he moved her off him and ensured her seat belt was fastened.

As if by unspoken agreement, once they

reached the palace they walked round the grounds towards Rohan's garden.

She was vaguely aware of the curious glances from people they passed. She and Rohan weren't touching but she was sure the tension in her body from the anticipation of soon being in his arms was radiating from her.

They barely stepped into the garden before turning to each other.

'I've missed you so much,' Rohan said.

Conversation seemed impossible when the urgency to kiss was so strong.

She'd missed him too. She had been trying to reconcile herself to never being with Rohan like this again. He'd really chosen her.

'Are you sure you want to do this?' she asked, finally managing to break apart and putting an arm's length distance between them.

'Of course I'm sure,' he replied as he drew her to him again.

She pushed him away. 'No, I don't mean that! Are you sure about your decision? You've chosen to be with me?'

Rohan laughed as he adjusted his clothing and took a few minutes to compose himself. He stared directly in her eyes and said, 'Yes, Priya Sen, I choose you.'

Tear's pricked Priya's eyes. The simplicity of his words made their truth undeniable.

'And your family won't mind you're not getting married yet,' she asked.

'What?' Rohan raised his eyebrows. 'Of course, I'm getting married.'

His admission was like a knife to her heart.

The glow on Priya's face faded. Rohan inwardly cursed himself for making such a pig's ear of everything. When he'd planned this day out, it seemed so romantic—arranging to meet in the place they first kissed.

He hadn't counted on how good it would feel to have Priya back in his arms, back where she belonged. He hadn't factored in how interminable the car ride back to the palace would be.

He'd initially thought when they arrived at the palace he would take her to the ballroom balcony to stand next to the pillar where they first met, but the need to be alone with Priya, where they wouldn't be interrupted was paramount so they came to his garden.

Once there, a conversation should have been their priority, but having the chance to draw Priya to him was too irresistible and from the moment he held her, he needed to kiss her like a thirsty plant needs water. Which was why he was in this mess, blurting things out without thinking.

'I'm sorry, I can't do that, Rohan,' Priya said moving away from him and wrapping her arms around herself. 'I'm sorry. I love you but I won't be your other woman for a few months while you're courting your future wife.'

The blood ran from his face as he realised how she'd interpreted his comments about getting married.

'No, Priya, no,' he said quickly. 'It's not what I meant. I don't want a relationship with you for a few more months.'

He couldn't mistake her hurt expression. Why was everything he said coming out wrong? Perhaps actions were louder than words in this scenario. He reached into his pocket and pulled out a small box.

Priya took a step away when he presented it to her.

'Rohan?' she said, shakily.

He opened the box displaying a kundan ring in a floral design with diamond petals around a central emerald.

'This is a family heirloom,' he explained. 'Each man presents it to his chosen bride and she holds on to it until it's ready to be passed on to the next generation. I asked my mother for it.'

Priya blinked, looking confused. He still wasn't doing this right. Smiling nervously as he looked directly into her eyes, Rohan bent onto one knee.

'Rohan,' Priya said, clutching her hands to her heart.

'Priya Sen. You are the love of my life. You're the reason I wake up in the morning and my last thought before I go to sleep. Please do me the greatest honour and make me the happiest man in the world. Will you marry me?' It wasn't the most eloquent proposal, but it was heartfelt. He held his breath.

She stared at him, as if making sure he was serious.

'Please,' he added.

Her lips lifted in an uncertain smile, then straightened again. She made a small sound, like a laugh of disbelief. Then as he continued to look at her, trying to convince her of his sincerity and silently begging her to say yes, her smile grew stronger.

She bit her lip, then nodded slowly at first, then faster as tears started to pour. 'Yes, Rohan. I'll marry you.'

He almost tripped in his haste to stand and embrace her.

A long while later they sat on the bench, Priya on his lap, gentle touches and kisses replacing the frantic passion of earlier.

'You'll need to think about who you want to invite to the wedding,' Rohan said.

'It's a bit soon for that isn't it?'

'Are you kidding? My mother's going to summon the pandit and the wedding coordinator as soon as we tell her we're getting married.'

Priya tensed next to him.

'I haven't met your parents yet. I can't meet them for the first time and tell them I'm marrying their son.'

'There's nothing to worry about. They're going to love you. I haven't met your father either,' Rohan pointed out. 'I'm just as nervous to see him to ask for his blessing to marry his beautiful, amazing daughter.'

She shrugged. 'Hopefully one day you will.'

'Are you thinking of inviting him to the wedding?'

'Of course I'll invite him. He is my father. I don't know if he'll attend—it'll probably depend on how busy he is. I don't need his attention or his approval. If he doesn't come, it will be his loss.'

Rohan wanted to cheer. 'Exactly. And what about your dadu and didima?' he asked, slowly.

Her smile was sad. 'I told you I don't know where they are. I don't know if they're alive.'

He expelled a breath. 'I do. I found them. They want to get back in touch with you desperately. It sounds like a lot of things happened in the background which they should tell you about. But they never wanted to break contact with you. I can bring them here if you want to see them.'

Priya hid her face against his chest. He could feel the dampness in his shirt.

'Thank you,' she mumbled. 'I can't believe you did that for me.' She lifted her head. 'No I can. It's just who you are as a person. No wonder I love you.'

'And I love you,' he said, kissing the tip of her nose. 'And your grandparents love you, and my parents will love you too.'

Priya gave a scared laugh. 'Your parents are the Maharaja and Maharani of Adysara. Oh, my goodness. This is so much to take in.' She bent forward holding her head in her hands. He could hear her trying to regulate her breathing.

'Everything okay?' he asked, gently moving her hair so he could see her profile. 'You're not thinking of changing your mind are you?'

'Maybe. No.' She sat up and stared intently at him. 'How are you going to tell your parents you want to marry me. A nobody. I don't bring anything with me.'

'You are enough.'

Priya convulsed with emotion. All her life she'd wanted to hear those words, never truly believing they would be true. But sitting on the bench, sitting in Rohan's embrace, she knew for Rohan it was true—she was enough.

'I already told my parents,' Rohan continued. 'They know I was planning to propose.'

'And they didn't try to talk you out of it?' She was still trying to wrap her head around the idea of marrying into the royal family of Adysara. 'Oh, Rohan. What about your duty and your family's expectations? I can't ask you to sacrifice everything you are for me.'

'There's no sacrifice. I have a duty to my people, but I also have a duty to myself. If I carried on searching for an advantageous match I would have been acting dishonourably because you're the only one I want as my wife. If I had to give up being yuvaraja I would because it would mean more to me to be your husband.'

He was turning her into a leaky tap.

'You're not being asked to give up your position?' Priya asked anxiously.

'I'm not. I'm still Yuvaraja, in line to become the next Maharaja of Adysara which I will reign over with my maharani.' He paused. 'Unless you want me to give it up. We can live a quiet life in England if that's what you prefer.'

Priya shook her head, staggered by the lengths Rohan was prepared to go to put what she wanted first. He'd contacted her grandparents—she never thought she'd see them again. But he made it happen because he thought about what would make her happy.

But her happiness was entwined with his.

She smiled. 'There's still a lot of the islands I haven't seen yet. And there's the murals and caves to preserve.'

Rohan laced his fingers through hers. 'My father said it's what you'll bring to the country—your skills in conservation which will help the regeneration and bring greater prosperity to us.'

Priya's laughter pealed out. It wasn't close to what the royal family must consider a real advantageous marriage, but it warmed her to know Rohan's parents were prepared to accept her as part of his life.

She bit her lip. 'Would it be appropriate for me to lead the work though, if I'm part of the royal family. It could be awkward for my team members to treat me the same as before.'

Rohan chuckled. 'You know we can sort through this kind of thing later. The only thing that matters is you love me and I love you and we're getting married. The rest can wait.'

She was about to relax back into Rohan's arms, but she said, 'Are you sure this is what you want?'

'I have never been more certain of anything.'

Priya didn't know when, if ever, she had felt so at peace, completely enveloped in love.

They sat in each other's arms in blissful peace until Rohan said, 'We should make some decisions before we tell my parents. Would you like to get married in England or here?' he asked. 'It's probably the first thing they'll need to know.'

It still sounded surreal to think about wedding details.

'We can get married in a register office, it it's what you want,' he continued.

'Oh, you're embarrassed to be seen with me, then,' she replied with a twinkle.

'What? Of course not. But I thought you wouldn't want the pomp and circumstance of an Adysarian royal wedding.'

'Well, it wouldn't be my first choice. If it was up to me we would elope tomorrow.'

He laughed. 'I'm open to that idea.'

Priya had no doubt Rohan would begin to arrange an elopement immediately if he thought it was what she really wanted.

'I love you. You are Yuvaraja of Adysara. Your people have been waiting for your wedding since you were born. As soon as the gala was over, it was all they talked about. The circumstances of our wedding wouldn't normally be important to me, but they're important to your people, which makes it important to you, which makes it important to me after all.' She grinned. 'I'm happy to get married here, with all the traditions and spectacle that involves. All that matters is I get to be your wife.'

'I love you for offering, but I know how you don't like being the centre of attention.'

She swallowed. 'I never felt I was worth being the centre of attention. I worried having the limelight on me would show everyone

how underserving I really was. You helped
me see that I have worth. You've given me
the confidence to take my day in the sun. I
would be proud to stand next to you in front
of all your people and become your wife.'

He kissed her deeply, making any further
conversation difficult and unnecessary.

EPILOGUE

Five years later

'AND THIS SECTION here required a special paste, which we had to mix ourselves, to stabilise the area before the conservation team could start work on it,' Priya said, indicating part of a recently restored mural in the grand dining room. 'Do you want to know what we used in the paste?'

'A little young to be your apprentice, isn't he?' Rohan's voice came from the doorway.

'Dada!' From her arms, her two-year-old stretched towards his father.

'Never too early to start an appreciation of the arts,' Priya said, lifting her face to Rohan's for his kiss as she transferred their son over to him.

'We should head back. Your dadu and didima are in our quarters waiting for this little man,' Rohan said as he nuzzled his son.

Priya's heart warmed, as it always did at the mention of her grandparents, not just because they were part of her life now, but their reappearance was a constant reminder of Rohan's love for her. Because he knew how much they meant to her, he'd gone to huge efforts to find them and then brought them to the island. Amidst many hugs and tears, they'd become reacquainted and Priya now completely understood why they'd fallen out of touch, but instead of dwelling on the past she wanted to concentrate on spending more time with them in the future. And shortly after their reunion, her dadu and didima had moved to Adysara permanently. Even though Priya's father had attended her wedding to Rohan four years ago, it was her grandparents who'd accompanied her down the aisle.

As they made their way back to their quarters, she watched Rohan and their son blow raspberries on each other's cheeks as they recited nursery rhymes. They looked like any happy father and child. But in two days they would be the Maharaja and Yuvaraja of Adysara.

'How did your meetings go?' she asked, once they'd left their son with her grandparents and were making their way to their private garden.

'Everything's going according to plan,' he

replied. He'd spent the day going through the final arrangements for the handover of power from his father.

She'd already had many practice sessions in the palace's great chamber, being directed on where she needed to stand and what actions to do on the day her husband was crowned. The day she would become the Maharani of Adysara. Sometimes it still felt like a dream.

They reached their garden and made their way to the bench where she took her usual place on Rohan's lap. Even though they no longer needed to meet in secret, they still escaped to the garden whenever they could. Or to cave six. Both places were special to them, but cave six was the first cave the conservation team had worked on and restored and it was a huge draw for tourists. Adysara's tourism industry was booming since Summer Palace Island had opened for business three years before and the island had already become one of the go-to luxury holiday destinations bringing wealth and investment to the country. Just as Rohan had predicted.

'I heard all hotels are at full capacity for the gala and coronation,' Priya said.

Rohan's smile was pure joy. 'It's worked out well,' he said in a true understatement.

'Perhaps we missed a trick having the gala

and your coronation in the same year—separate events would have optimised the number of tourists.'

Rohan laughed then was silent a moment. 'My coronation. In a way I've been preparing for this since I was child, but now it's only days away I don't think I'm ready.'

She wrapped her arms around him in a comforting hug. 'Of course you are. You always have been. But if you'd like I can have a quiet word with your dad, persuade him not to abdicate,' she said with a cheeky grin.

'Well, if anyone can, you can. You have both my parents wrapped around your little finger, the same as you have me. And not just us. The whole country too.'

Priya bit her lip. It wasn't the first time Rohan had pointed out how the people of Adysara felt about her, but after growing up not feeling loved or wanted, she was only slowly coming round to the idea it was true. It had been through Rohan's love that she had begun to believe that it was possible that she was cared for by so many people. He made no secret of how much he adored her—making it obvious to the world he never regretted his decision to choose her as his wife.

'I love you so much, Rohan.' Her words were simple but heartfelt.

'And I love you,' Rohan replied, lifting her mouth to his.

Even now, five years after she'd first come to the island and fallen in love with its prince, she sometimes had to remind herself she wasn't going to wake up from this fairy-tale life. But Rohan's love for her was real, deep and everlasting—the same as her love for him. And they would live a long, happy life together, full of love.

* * * * *

If you enjoyed this story, check out this other great read from Ruby Basu

Baby Surprise for the Millionaire

Available now!